I Will Open My Mouth in Parables

*Taradiddles and Tales
of My West Virginia Home*

Fictional Short Stories

Richard Smith

Published By ScriptSmith
ScriptSmith.com
Copyright © 2013 Richard Smith
ISBN-13: 978-1490422978
ISBN-10: 1490422978

The cover photograph, "The Great Flood," is of downtown
Quick, WV, in the spring of 1961. The lady with the
umbrella is Corba Quick Mullins, whose ancestors founded
the town. The photo was taken by the author's father,
Richard Smith, Sr.

I Will Open My Mouth in Parables

Matthew 13:35

So was fulfilled what was spoken through the prophet: "I will open my mouth in parables, I will utter things hidden since the creation of the world."

Dedication

To my father, who provided a home, and to my mother who made it a worthwhile place to live.

My Native Land
Sir Walter Scott

Breathes there the man, with soul so dead,
Who never to himself hath said,
This is my own, my native land!
Whose heart hath ne'er within him burn'd,
As home his footsteps he hath turn'd
From wandering on a foreign strand!

Contents

⪧⪦⪧⪦⪧⪦

Best When Read Aloud

JOSHUA

18 Now the birth of Jesus Christ was on this wise: When as his mother Mary was espoused to Joseph, before they came together, she was found with child of the Holy Ghost.

19 Then Joseph her husband, being a just man, and not willing to make her a public example, was minded to put her away privily.

20 But while he thought on these things, behold, the angel of the Lord appeared unto him in a dream, saying, Joseph, thou son of David, fear not to take unto thee Mary thy wife: for that which is conceived in her is of the Holy Ghost.

21 And she shall bring forth a son, and thou shalt call his name Jesus: for he shall save his people from their sins.

Matthew 1: 18 - 21
King James Version

IT WAS DURING one of those periodic phone calls home that my mom said something about Aunt Harriette. I don't remember exactly what she said; just some passing reference, but it certainly brought back a flood of memories. Aunt Harriette was actually my great-aunt, my great-grandmother's sister. She was a very spirited woman, as were all the women in her family. She was also very religious, which had a tremendous effect on my life, as well as the lives of everyone in my family. But I guess there's one very significant event (at least for me) that I'll always remember when I think of Aunt Harriette.

It happened the year I was in the ninth grade at Quick Elementary and Junior High School, the same year that Mary Anne came to Quick to live with her Aunt Virginia. We had all heard about Mary Anne from our parents, (mostly from our mothers), or from Aunt Harriette. Mary Anne was a Disgrace. She had shamed her family, she had shamed her friends, and she had shamed herself.

Rumor had it that the baby was due about the middle of January; that as soon as it was born, it would be adopted by a childless couple from Charleston, and that Mary Anne would never be allowed to see the baby. "It'll be better for her if she never sees it," Aunt Harriette told us. "That way she won't be so attached to it."

The topic of Mary Anne's disgrace was usually the prelude to longer, more serious lectures on a series of evils from the failure to obey our parents to "running with the wrong crowd."

After hearing so much about Mary Anne, we were all eager to get a good look at her that first day, as she entered ninth grade at Quick Junior High. She dressed plainly, never smiled, and always kept her eyes down. Mary Anne bore her shame well.

Mary Anne was a little on the plump side, but not really "fat" in those days before "Twiggy" and all the thinness mania that later engulfed our society. She was not particularly attractive and she really didn't look all that pregnant. I mean, if you didn't already know, you would never have guessed.

In the spirit of small town Christian charity, we kept our distance from Mary Anne. Not because we didn't like her, but because it was traditional to keep your distance from anyone new. More than that, none of us wanted word to get home to our parents, or to Aunt Harriette, that we were seen associating with a known teenage soon-to-be unwed mother.

However, fate being as it is, it became difficult for me to escape associating with such an unsavory character. Because of the tendency of the teachers at Quick Junior High to seat people in alphabetical order and due to the fact that we were a very small ninth grade class, Mary Anne sat directly in front of me in Home Room and in all of the other classes that we attended together.

This quirk of fate won me a lot of unwanted teasing and I was always looking for ways to deflect it. I'm not trying to excuse myself, but that may be why I said what I said that started all the trouble and got me into a great deal of hot water, especially with my Aunt Harriette.

It was the middle of November. Mary Anne had just celebrated her fifteenth birthday and by this time she definitely looked pregnant. As much as possible under the circumstances, we had accepted her into our society at Quick Junior High School. Mary Anne was a good student and as we began to open up to her, she began to open up to us. We discovered that she was actually a very nice person, in spite of being a Disgrace.

I had actually begun to think of her as "okay-looking." Under different circumstances, of course, I may have even considered asking her to go to Fred Shamblin's Dairy Bar on a Friday night.   But under the *current* circumstances, I had to watch my step very carefully. If I were so much as seen talking to her, all the guys would begin calling me "Daddy." (The teasing was instigated by my best friend, fellow ninth grader, and uncle, Ron.) To make matters worse, my brother Larry would make sure that Aunt Harriette was kept fully informed about Mary Anne, especially if there was even the slightest connection to me. And, in some cases, Larry's account of an incident made the connection much clearer than it might have otherwise been.

So, at the meeting of the ninth grade Annual Christmas Festival Committee, I opened my mouth and that's when the trouble began. We were planning the school's Christmas activities. In those days, it was not illegal to pray in school, so no one gave it a second thought when the school sponsored an annual Christmas Pageant.

There were five of us on the committee. Mrs. Hawkins, a gentle person who had been my second and third grade teacher, was our sponsor. We met during lunch period to plan this year's Festival.

Several ideas were suggested by various members of the committee. For the most part, they were stale repeats of the same type of pageants that had taken place for as long as I could remember. But, since no one seemed to have a better idea, we tried to think of ways to put a breath of freshness into the stale ideas. Then my good friend (and one of my tormentors) Frankie Hamilton came up with an idea that really seemed to catch on.

"Why don't we do a live Christmas pageant with real animals and everything?"

Everyone liked the idea of real animals and before long we were organizing the greatest Christmas Festival that Quick had ever seen, or would ever see again. We would set up a manger on the school lawn and act out the events of that First Night in scripture and song.

We'd bring in real animals, have Shepherds (no sheep though, because no one around Quick raised sheep), Angels, Wise Men, lots of scripture readings, and tons of Christmas carols. After that, we'd go inside the school for hot chocolate and cookies. It sounded great!

Then came the neatest idea of all. Why not have a parade. We'd have Mary and Joseph lead the parade, followed by the Angels (singing, of course), then the Shepherds (maybe singing), and finally the three Wise Men (probably not singing).

The more we talked the more ideas we came up with. Finally it was settled. We would march through Quick singing Christmas carols until we reached the school. Then we would act out the night of Jesus' birth in song and scripture. The steps and the large cement porch that lead into the school would be our stage.

The ninth graders would get the leading roles; the speaking parts and other roles of importance such as being one of the Three Wise Men. Anyone else who wanted to be in the play could be Angels or Shepherds. The boys would be Shepherds and the girls would be Angels. (In those days, Angels were thought to be women, with the possible exceptions of the Archangel Michael and arch villain Lucifer.) After the enactment, we'd go inside for refreshments. Great!

It was then, when we began to discuss who would be who in the pageant, that I said what I said. I meant it as a joke, a vain attempt to thwart some of the teasing.

"Why not let Mary Anne be the mother of Jesus?" I asked. "She certainly looks the part."

I thought they'd laugh, or groan, or at least tell me that it was "mean" to suggest such a thing. But they didn't. Instead, they turned and looked at me. I felt my face turning red.

"Why, Richard," said Mrs. Hawkins. "That's a wonderful idea!"

And, can you believe it? Everyone else agreed. What I had intended as a joke – as a way of deflating my tormentors – became a joke on me, especially when *I* was selected for the role of Joseph!

The rest of the group excitedly continued planning the Festival, but I sat there staring at the desk. It was all over for me! I knew as soon as the meeting ended, Frankie would head straight for Ron and tell him what had happened. I knew that I was in for an unmerciful amount of teasing. I was doomed.

What I didn't know then was that the thing I worried about the most was only the tip of an iceberg.

The first hint of the coming storm appeared on the horizon about a week later. After church on Sunday, Aunt Harriette asked me if it was true that Mary Anne was really going to be Mary the Mother of Jesus in the school's Christmas pageant.

"Yes," I told her. But I deliberately failed to mention who was going to be Joseph.

(Thanks to Larry, I'm sure she not only knew that I was to be Joseph, but that I'm the one who suggested that Mary Anne be Mary.)

Then, just after the Thanksgiving holiday, a rumor circulated around the school that a group of women and two ministers from the community were meeting with the principal; something about being unhappy with the Christmas Pageant. I don't know why, but I didn't think much about it until the planning committee was asked to reconvene.

When we met, (this time without Mrs. Hawkins), Mr. Robertson, the principal, told us that there was a problem and he needed our help to solve it.

Mr. Robertson was a very religious man. He attended a church that did not believe in having musical instruments as part of the worship. He kept this practice in effect at Quick Junior High and taught us to sing *a capella*. This was a new dimension for us, one which we all enjoyed (although most of us guys would never admit it).

All the students felt Mr. Robertson was very fair. He gave everyone the same number of "licks" when he paddled us, and he ran the school with an even hand. I guess you'd say that he was consistent. He did what he said he would do, and we knew it. So we liked Mr. Robertson and wanted to help him solve the problem.

We were all taken aback (at least I was) when he told us the problem was our choice for

Mary in the Christmas Pageant. Would we be willing to change our minds?

My first thought was that God truly was good and merciful, and that He does indeed answer prayer. Now, he was about to rescue me from the pit which I had dug with my own tongue.

Mr. Robertson looked at us and we looked at him, then we looked at each other. It was very clear from the looks on our faces how we felt about the matter, but nobody spoke. There was a somewhat long and uncomfortable silence.

"No sir," I heard a familiar voice say. "We're not willing to change our minds."

I was surprised to recognize the voice as my own.

I looked at the others and they nodded their agreement.

"We selected Mary Anne and we're sticking with our choice," I said. "I mean, how would it make her feel if we changed our minds now? She's suffered enough." I looked at Frankie. I wanted to say "And so have I" but I didn't.

Mr. Robertson asked if everyone agreed, and everyone said they did. Then something happened that surprised me. Mr. Robertson smiled.

"Mrs. Hawkins was right," he told us. "She said you wouldn't change your minds."

Then he sighed.

"Okay. I'm with you. But I can tell you that we're in for a bumpy ride."

Actually, he was wrong. There was only one bump. It came about a week later, in the form of an announcement that the Quick Junior High School Annual Christmas Festival for that year had been canceled, by order of the Kanawha County Board of Education.

Mr. Robertson again asked to meet with the committee. This time, Mrs. Hawkins joined him.

"We did the best we could," she told us. "You would have been proud of how Mr. Robertson handled the situation. But the opposition was just too strong."

"We'll have the pageant anyway," I pronounced.

"Okay. But not on school property," said Mr. Robertson.

"We'll find another place," said Frankie.

"Right," chimed in the group.

"You don't know what you're up against with this group," said Mrs. Hawkins.

"Who are these people anyway?" I asked.

There was a sudden chilly silence. I looked around at the group, but no one was looking back at me.

"You don't know?" asked Mr. Robertson.

"No!"

"It's a group of about thirty people. (ten percent of the population of Quick). They include ministers from the Holiness Church of

I Will Open My Mouth In Parables

Christ and the Church of the Nazarene (my own minister!) and members of those two churches, and some from the Methodist church."

"Richard," said Mrs. Hawkins, "your mother is part of the group."

"My mother!"

"And," said Mr. Robertson, "your Aunt Harriette is the ring-leader!"

I felt like a fool. How could I have been so naive? How could this be happening without me even knowing about it? I looked at the other members of the group. So that was it. They all knew what I hadn't known; and they had kept the secret from me.

"All right, are you guys with me?" I asked.

"I am," said Frankie. "And you can count on the rest of the guys."

"I'm in," said another member of the group.

"Me too," said a fourth.

We were all in; and we were spoiling for a fight!

The committee began to revise its plans. We subdivided the tasks: Some people would plan for the refreshments, some would find the animals, some would make arrangements for getting costumes, and we'd all work on scripting the pageant.

My job was to find a place to have the pageant.

"Me!"

"This is your idea!"

I thought about the options. The school was ideal. The steps and porch made a wonderful outdoor stage. We needed some place like that. I thought about using the side of a hill, sort of a Pageant on the Mount, I guess. We certainly had plenty of hills in the area, but they were all too steep, and none was really very convenient. The only other possibility I could think of was the Methodist church. It was conveniently located in "downtown" Quick, across the street from the school. It had steps and a porch very similar to what was at the school. But some of the Methodists were against the pageant. Still, it might be worth a try.

I called the minister of the Methodist church. He didn't live in the community and was considered an outsider by most of his parishioners. I felt that this might be in our favor. Also, he wasn't part of the group that had vetoed our plans for the pageant. And, to add more weight to our side of the scale, he was young and might be more sympathetic toward what the young people of the community wanted to do. Even better (for us, at least), he was known to be "liberal." (His wife wore lipstick, even in church.)

When the minister answered the phone, I explained who I was and why I was calling. He had indeed heard of our plight, and he agreed that, as far as he was concerned, we could present the pageant on the steps and porch of the church. We could also serve refreshments in the basement. I was elated.

"But," he warned, "I'll have to get approval of the governing board."

That statement brought me crashing back to earth.

"The board meets this Thursday night. I'll call you Friday."

"It might be better if I call you," I suggested.

At noon on Friday I sneaked into the principal's office while Mr. Robertson was at lunch and dialed the Methodist minister's number. He answered too quickly.

"Uh . . . I, this is Richard . . . uh, Smith."

"Oh, hi Richard."

I waited, hoping that he would just tell me the results of the meeting. He didn't.

"I was calling about the pageant."

"Oh. Right!" I had a feeling he was teasing me. "Well, we had quite a meeting. You should have been there."

"I'm in enough trouble the way it is."

He laughed.

"That's what I hear. Say, that great-aunt of yours is a very . . . 'forceful' person."

"'Intimidating' is the word."

"Right! She's said some really nasty things about our church's spiritual condition and about the very slim chances of some of the church's members, including the minister, ever being admitted through the Pearly Gates!"

"I'm sure she has," I said. (In fact, I'd heard quite a few of her statements regarding the Methodists and their liberal minister. But I didn't feel it was appropriate to repeat them at the moment.)

"Well, to show that we Methodists are not ones to hold grudges, we voted to allow her nephew to hold a Christmas Pageant on our porch."

"Well, Praise the Lord," I said. And I meant it.

"I have to warn you though, not everyone was in favor of it. It was only a simple majority vote. But I think the church as a whole is very sympathetic to your cause, and especially your refusal to back down on the choice of Mary Anne as the Mother of Jesus. Very ingenious, I must admit."

"Uh . . . well, thanks."

"Your idea, I hear."

"Well, uh . . . yes."

"Another thing in your favor is that her aunt Virginia is one of our members. Hasn't attended since I came here, but she's still on the roll."

I told the minister how much we appreciated what he had done for us.

"God bless you," he said.

"Thanks."

"I probably should say 'God have mercy on your soul.'"

I tried to laugh, but the truth of his statement was too real. Even if we did pull this

Christmas pageant off, I'd still have to deal with great-aunt Harriette for the rest of my life (or at least for the rest of her life)

I hung up the phone and went to tell the others the good news. We were flying high. We were going to have our Christmas Pageant and no one was going to stop us now!

The last day of school before the Christmas holiday was December 22, only two days before Christmas Eve, the night we had chosen for the pageant. It was a festive day. The students were in high spirits. Everyone was smiling. I'd never seen so many happy people. There was a sense of unity in the school. We had wanted something and we were going to get it. It was the classic case of good versus evil, and it was clear to us which side we were on.

I met Mary Anne on the way to the temporary building that housed our home room. It had been "temporary" for about seven years.

"Merry Christmas," I said cheerfully.

Her eyes filled with tears. "I need to talk to you."

Uh-oh. We walked to the side of the building, out of the way of foot traffic.

"What's wrong?"

"I can't be in the Christmas Pageant."

"What?"

"Aunt Virginia forbids it." Tears rolled down her face. "She said that it's your way of making fun of my . . . 'condition.'"

Ouch!

"But, I . . . I'm . . . ."

"I don't mean 'you,' personally. I mean everyone."

"Mary Anne, believe me, it's not."

"I know," she sobbed. Suddenly she threw her arms around me. I could feel the big lump low in her abdomen between us. "You've been so wonderful to me."

Out of the corner of my eye I caught a glimpse of Ron and Frankie headed toward the classroom. Those two always seemed to be in the right place at the wrong time. I was sure I'd be hearing "Daddy" a lot before this day was over. But, to my surprise, they walked by, pretending not to notice.

Mary Anne stepped back. "If I go against Aunt Virginia, she says she'll send me home. I can't go back now. If . . . if I have to go back, it'd . . . they'd . . . it'd be so humiliating."

She began to shake with sobs as she dug into the pocket of her coat for a hanky.

"She's already told my folks that if I'm in the pageant, they'll have to come and get me."

We stood there; me looking at her, she looking at the ground.

"I'm so sorry!" she sobbed. "I just keep messing everything up."

She leaned forward against me. I put my arms around her shoulders. She's been through enough, I thought to myself; don't make her go through more.

"Listen," I said. "Don't worry. It'll work out."

"This has all been so awful. I didn't want a baby. I just wanted someone to love me. He said he loved me. What a lie!"

"Mary Anne. Don't."

"And I'll never even get to see my baby. And now I have to give up the only thing that made it even remotely meaningful . . . the chance for him to be the baby Jesus."

If she kept this up, I was going to cry.

"Mary Anne. It's okay."

"No it's not!" She pulled away and looked at me, tears running down her cheeks. "I won't let them do it. I won't let them take away my baby's chance to be somebody . . . to represent somebody so beautiful and pure. I don't care what happens!"

"Mary Anne, don't do something that's going to cause you even more pain."

"I don't care, Richie. I want this . . . for my baby."

"But he . . . it . . . will never know."

"I'll know."

"Think about it," I pled. "Please."

Her face softened. "I will." She smiled. She certainly was a pretty girl after all.

"I'm going to the restroom," she said.

"Why would her aunt do this?" I asked Ron at lunch.

"Family," he replied.

"Family?"

"Virginia was a Robinson."

So that was it. My great-aunt Harriette had also been a Robinson; before she married Martin Strickland. Foiled again. Aunt Harriette had gotten to Virginia and put pressure on her to keep Mary Anne out of the pageant. And it had worked. Or at least it had almost worked.

"The question is not 'why,'" said Frankie. "The question is 'what are we going to do if she doesn't show up?'"

"We can always find someone for the role of Mary," I said. "If nothing else . . ." I was fumbling for something with dramatic flair. "If nothing else, we'll walk the pony through Quick without a rider, just to make our point."

We were silent for a moment.

"What worries me most," I said, "is what happens if she *does* show up. We can't let her do this to herself."

After classes were out, almost everyone in the school met to talk about the pageant. By this time most of them had heard about Aunt Virginia's refusal to allow Mary Anne to be in the pageant.

"She says she'll be there, right?" asked one of the Wise Men.

"Right," I said.

"Then what's the problem?"

"The problem is, she gets sent home and everyone in her community finds out about the baby."

"Don't you think they already know?"

"No," said Carol, our lead Angel. "She told me the man who did it is married to her sister. Nobody knows but the family."

We were shocked by that bit of information and stood in stunned silence. Finally, I spoke.

"Jean. You'll be Mary."

"No," she said. "If Mary Anne can't do it, then we should do what you said. We should walk the pony through Quick with no rider."

"And no singing," someone in the back said. "We should make a statement."

And so it came to pass that it was decided we would not have a Mary the Mother of Jesus, nor a baby-to-be to represent the holy child, because there were those among us who felt that an unwed mother and her fatherless child reflected poorly on such a holy event.

The sad thing was that, if the truth were known, most of us felt the same way. But we knew Mary Anne. We knew the humiliation that she was suffering, and we wanted to honor her for that.

On Sunday, December 24, formerly "Pageant Day," but now "Statement Day," I went to church with the very people who fought most against what I was doing. I thought it was hypocritical of them to do what they were doing without once saying anything directly to me. But then I remembered that I was doing the same thing. Communication, the two-way street, was definitely closed . . . maybe never to reopen.

All the teens and even some of the younger kids sat together on the last rows of chairs. We were already making our statement. There we were, united in a cause for the good of mankind (actually, womankind too). We sang louder than usual. In fact, we usually didn't sing at all.

At the end of the sermon, the minister served communion; a ceremony that the Quick Church of the Nazarene only observed a couple times a year. The minister had arranged to have ushers direct the rows of worshipers to come forward, a new custom for him.

Then, after most of the adults and a few of the children who were sitting with their parents had been served, the minister closed the communion. He said, without looking at the back row, that he could not, in good conscience, allow people to participate who were not worthy of the blood and body of Christ. He referred to a statement in First Corinthians, Chapter Eleven, as support.

So, finally it was in the open. War had officially been declared, no doubt at the insistence of my great-aunt Harriette. But, for me, it was no longer a case of good versus evil, or even good versus good. It was "those in power" against "those who have no power."

As we stood for the dismissal prayer, I prayed only that Mary Anne would be safe.

Long before it began to get dark that evening, we started gathering in the field at the west edge of Quick that had been designated as our staging area. Every kid in Quick was there, and quite a few others who lived in Sanderson, out on Dutch Ridge, or in other areas nearby, but who attended Quick Junior High School.

We were very subdued. We brought candles and flashlights. We were ready to make our statement.

By 5:30, when Curtis Johnson arrived, bringing the pony on whose back Mary the Mother of Jesus would not ride, it was dark. At 5:45, fifteen minutes before our appointed departure time, the last kids arrived and joined our silent group. Candles were lit, and we sat, costumed, in an eerie glow and an equally eerie silence.

I looked at my watch. 5:55. I stood. Everyone stood. I walked to where Curtis waited with the pony. Everyone began forming a line behind the pony. Lead Angel Carol handed me a flowing white silky cloth she had brought, and I draped it over the riderless pony.

Just then, I felt someone touch my arm. I turned. I don't know where she came from, but there she stood. It was Mary Anne.

"What are you doing here?" I whispered.

"Help me up," she said.

"I can't let you do this."

"Help me up!" she demanded

"Mary Anne. No."

She turned to some of the shepherds.

"Help me up," she said to them.

Three Shepherds gently lifted her sidesaddle onto the pony. She looked at me and smiled.

"Let's go," she said. "We don't want to keep them waiting."

Curtis took the pony's bridle and started down the road toward Quick. I walked beside the pony next to Mary Anne.

"Let's sing," I said to Carol. And we did.

> Angels we have heard on high,
> Sweetly singing o'er the plains,
> And the mountains in reply,
> Echoing their joyous strains.

A capella. Mr. Robertson would have been proud.

We sang so loud that I'm sure we could be heard in Coco, Pinch, and Elkview, maybe even as far away as Big Chimney!

As the parade made its way down the main street (really, pretty much the only street) of Quick, some of the townspeople came out to cheer us on our way. And, to my surprise, a lot of them joined our march.

When we rounded the curve and headed toward the center of Quick, we could see that people were already gathered at the Methodist church. On we marched. Louder we sang. Something was up. I didn't know what. I just prayed that whatever it was, we'd be able to handle it without Mary Anne getting hurt.

As we neared the church, I had the opportunity to look the situation over. It only took a moment for me to scope it out and realize that ecumenicity had come to Quick. There before us was a group of people that included the ministers of the other two churches, as well as prominent members of all three churches. These people, who under other circumstances would never be caught dead speaking to each other, had joined forces against the Devil (me) and his motley band. The ministers and church members had mounted the stairs and porch of the Methodist church in order to keep us from having our pageant there.

As we drew close, I could see that the group was primed for a confrontation. I decided to do my best to disappoint them – for Mary Anne's sake and for mine. My plan was to have our pageant in the street. I knew they'd sing to try to drown us out, and when they did, we'd simply sing the same songs they were singing. I thought it was a great plan, but before I could enact it, someone called out: "Get off the porch," and the confrontation had begun.

As we came to the porch and stopped, my eyes met those of their "ringleader." She seemed intent on burning a hole through me. It took all the strength I could muster, but I smiled at her. Then I turned my attention to my mother, who was standing next to her. I smiled at her too.

"Hi, Mom," I said.

A ripple of laughter went through the crowd and the tension was broken.

I turned to the group behind me to tell them we'd hold the pageant right where we stood when someone on the porch began shouting something about abominations and desecrating God's holy place. I fought hard to control my emotions. But then someone said "She has no right to blaspheme the Holy Ghost by acting like the mother of the Lord Jesus Christ."

I whirled back toward the steps. I was angry and I shouted the first thing that popped into my mind. I don't even know where I got the idea, but I said "She's just like another woman we all know: fifteen years old, pregnant, and unmarried."

The crowd went silent. For a moment, people tried to figure out who I was talking about. Then it dawned on them: Mary, the mother of Jesus. She was young, pregnant, and unwed.

Carl Dixon, who, because of his booming baritone voice had been designated as our Scripture Reader, began reading the passage in the Gospel of Matthew about how Mary became pregnant and about the Angel who came to Joseph and told him about the special baby that was to be born.

But as the confrontation was being played out, another drama of even greater proportions was taking place in the lives of the two "ringleaders" at the scene. When I said what I did about someone who was fifteen, pregnant, and unmarried, my great-aunt had been looking away from me, toward someone else. But when she heard it, she immediately turned back to face me and her eyes flashed with anger. It was at that moment that I thought of something that had completely slipped my mind. And, if I had remembered it before I said what I said about young, pregnant, and unwed, I would never have said it.

When I was growing up, I lived with my parents in "downtown" Quick. But I did a lot of work on my Grandparent's farm; my dad's mother and father. About two years ago, I had also done some work for my great-uncle Jake Robinson, Aunt Harriette's brother. Each afternoon for three days, I walked two miles from my grandparent's farm to Jake Robinson's place and worked there until dark.

Uncle Jake was having a problem with high blood pressure and had been having fainting spells. The doctor told him he was to stay inside out of the heat and not to do any strenuous work.

Aunt Harriette had asked me to go over and help out and by the time I got there, the weeds in Jake's vegetable garden were knee high.

Jake was, to put it mildly, "thrifty," and the hoe he gave me to use must have been the original iron hoe, dating to about the time of the cavemen. It was a heavy, very blunt instrument mounted on the end of a homemade handle. It was too dull to cut the weeds, so I had to beat them until they eventually broke. If I raised the hoe to any height at all, so I could bring it down with enough force to pierce the ground, the head would come loose and slide down the handle toward my hands.

During the afternoon of the third day I worked for Jake, Aunt Harriette came to visit. They came out so she could say hello and give me some pointers on how to hoe a garden in her typical "know it all" fashion. Then she and Jake went inside for a visit. An hour or so later, Harriette left, and Jake came out to the garden. I could tell he was not in the best of moods.

He watched me work for a while, and then began to complain about how slow I was and what a poor job I was doing. I had known Jake all my life, and this certainly didn't seem like him. I was afraid his blood pressure might be up and he was about to have a stroke. After a few moments, he grabbed the hoe and said "Here, let me show you how to hoe a garden."

On Jake's first attempt, the head of the iron hoe came loose and slid down the handle nearly smashing his fingers. On the down stroke, Jake drove the hoe-less handle into the ground. After saying a word or two that were certainly not heard in church circles, Jake pounded the end of the handle on the ground to try to get the head to stay in place.

On his second attempt, he sliced off one of his best newly blooming tomato plants, about three inches above the ground. This time he let forth a whole barrage of words and expressions rarely heard in those days, but which are today commonly used on television and in the movies, threw the hoe on the ground, and started toward the house. Then he stopped and started back toward me. He was really angry and I thought he might hit me.

"That woman and her 'holier-than-thou' attitude drive me crazy!" He was practically shouting. "I'd like to take that hoe handle and . . . ."

Fortunately he regained his composure before he provided me with any sort of vivid description of what he'd like to do with that hoe handle.

"She goes around telling everyone else how they should live. She thinks she's so much better than the rest of us. Well, let me tell you something."

He took a few steps toward me.

"If people really knew the truth about her . . . ." He walked even closer. "No one knows the family secret. But I know. And sometimes I feel like telling everyone, just to see her squirm."

Jake looked around as if checking to see if anyone else was present. He leaned toward me.

"When she was about your age . . . fifteen, she got to running round with the wrong crowd. Mom tried to rein her in, but she'd crawl out the window late at night and sneak off. And guess what? She got . . . she got . . . you know," he made a motion toward his stomach. "You know, in a family way."

"Pregnant" was not a word that was said out loud in those days, especially among men.

It was certainly shocking news about Aunt Harriette, but I tried not to show it.

Jake seemed to be regaining some of his composure.

"I guess she was lucky in a way that she couldn't carry it. And it did straighten her out. But it doesn't give her the right to come out here and tell me how I should live my life!"

Jake turned and stormed to the house. He slammed the door so hard, I was afraid that it would fall off the hinges.

I finished the garden that afternoon and went to the house to tell Jake I was done. He had completely regained his composure and paid me, in cash, the agreed upon fifty cents an hour. Then he gave me an extra half dollar and told me what a good job I had done. As I turned to leave, he called my name.

"Listen," he said. "Don't mention what I told you out there," he pleaded. "If she ever found out . . . ." He looked very anxious. He didn't need to say any more. I knew exactly what he meant.

"My lips are sealed," I promised.

Now, a year and a half later, I stood in front of the Methodist church shouting about someone who was "fifteen, pregnant, and unmarried," and watching as a look of horror come over Aunt Harriette's face. And in that moment, another drama began to be played out – one that I only now truly understand.

Aunt Harriette's secret had been safe all these years. No one knew but Uncle Jake and he died last summer. Since it was a secret and since I could not possibly have known about it, Aunt Harriette took my words to be the voice of God speaking to her. She began to cry.

A deep hush settled over the group as people watched this seventy-two-year-old woman weep. The only voice to be heard was that of Carl Dixon as he read from the Gospel of Matthew. When he looked up and saw Aunt Harriette crying, he stopped in mid-sentence.

Aunt Harriette looked at me, then at Mary Anne. Next, she turned to my mother.

"Come on, Shirley," she said, loud enough for just about everyone to hear. "We're in the wrong place."

She took mom by the arm and they started down the steps. None of us could believe what was happening. It was truly a miracle of God!

At the foot of the steps, Aunt Harriette stopped by the pony. She reached out and took Mary Anne by the hand.

"God bless you, child," she whispered, "and God bless that little baby you're carrying." Then she came over and stood beside me.

We sang "Joy to the World!" Then we sang every Christmas carol we knew. We sang them all at least once and some, like Silent

Night, we sang twice. We sang and sang and sang. And as we sang, the people on the porch slowly melted away. Some joined us in song and others sneaked out of the crowd and fled to the safety of their homes.

Finally, someone said, "I'm freezing," and we all realized that it had gotten very cold. We decided it was time to serve the hot chocolate that was waiting for us in the basement.

Most of the kids hurried down the stairs into the basement and most of the adults headed home. But there was a lot of handshaking and even some hugging (not a usual occurrence among Quickonians) as the spirit of love and Christmas filled our hearts to overflowing.

I stood there next to Mom and Aunt Harriette while the others were leaving. After a moment, Aunt Harriette smiled.

"You're not such a bad kid after all," she said. I knew that was the equivalent of her saying "I'm sorry, I love you, and I'm proud of you" all in one.

The teenagers spent another hour enjoying each other's friendship before Aunt Virginia said that it was time to take Mary Anne home. One look at Mary Anne told us Virginia was right. She was obviously very tired.

We all gathered around her. We had a lot we wanted to say, but we didn't know how to say it. Some of the girls hugged her while most of us guys just stood around and looked concerned. As she started to leave, she turned to us, and with tears in her eyes, thanked us for everything we had done and said how special it was for her and for her baby. Then she looked me right in the face, smiled, turned, and walked out the door. I never saw her again.

It was just after nine o'clock when I got home from the church. The phone was ringing. It was a somewhat frantic Aunt Virginia. She was trying to find Harriette, who, in those days, didn't have a telephone. Aunt Harriette had volunteered to serve as Mary Anne's midwife and Aunt Virginia wanted to let her know that the baby was on its way. I told Virginia that I'd drive up to Harriette's place and bring her back.

"Hurry," she said. "It won't be long now."

I jumped into mom's 1949 Mercury and drove furiously east out of Quick to Aunt Harriette little house. I told her about Mary Anne and the baby. We hurried to the car and headed back toward Quick.

Most of the trip we rode in silence, but as we neared Virginia's house, I turned to Aunt Harriette.

"You volunteered to be the midwife?" I asked.

"Yeah. I've got a lot of experience, you know."

"Just when did you volunteer," I teased.

"Oh, I was planning on it all along, but I didn't say anything official 'till tonight."

I grinned at her and she grinned back. Being there when the baby was born was her way of making amends for the things she said about Mary Anne. Like most of us in the family, the only way she could say "I'm sorry" was by doing something for the person she felt she had wronged. But, she really was the one who should be there. She was the most experienced midwife in the area.

We pulled up in front of the house. I looked at Aunt Harriette.

"Should I come in?" I asked.

"You'd just be in the way," Aunt Harriette said. She opened the door and got out. Then she looked back in at me.

"Don't worry. I'll handle it just the way the Lord wants it handled," she said and closed the door. As I drove slowly home I couldn't help but wonder what she had meant by that.

The couple who were going to adopt the baby arrived just minutes before he was born. All the preparations were made (plenty of hot water, I guess) and everything went smoothly. Just after the baby was born, Aunt Harriette took him away, to check him over and clean him up. The couple waited anxiously and Mary Anne lay in the bed sobbing her heart out for the baby she would never see.

Then Aunt Harriette did what it was that she evidently felt that the Lord wanted done. After the baby was clean and ready, she took him back into the room with Mary Anne and closed the door. No one knows what went on behind that door and when asked, Aunt Harriette just smiles and changes the subject.

Those outside could hear some whispering, some crying, some laughing, and some silence. About half an hour later, the door opened and Aunt Harriette and the baby emerged. Harriette carried the baby over to the very anxious couple, held him out to them, then suddenly pulled the baby back.

"She has one request," Aunt Harriette said. Then she waited.

The woman turned and looked anxiously at her husband. Then she turned back to Aunt Harriette. "What is it?" the woman said fearfully.

"She wants you to promise that you'll name the baby 'Joshua.'"

The couple looked at each other, then at Aunt Harriette. They felt that without that promise they would never get the baby.

"Okay," said the woman.

Aunt Harriette looked down at the baby for a full minute, and then she looked up, first at the woman, then at the man.

"I have your word then that the baby will be named Joshua."

"You have our word," said the man.

Aunt Harriette handed the baby to the woman.

"What a wonderful Christmas present," the woman said; then she began to cry.

Mary Anne's parents came for her two days after the baby was born. We . . . I had hoped for a chance to say goodbye, but her parents were in a hurry. We thought maybe Mary Anne would come back to visit us or Aunt Virginia, but as far as I know, she never did.

About the middle of January, Mr. Robertson read a note to our homeroom class from Mary Anne's mother. In an almost unfriendly way, she thanked us for being Mary Anne's friends and said the whole incident had left some very deep scars. She asked us not to write, even if Mary Anne wrote to us. She said it was necessary, if Mary Anne was to get over the trauma, but it was easy to read the embarrassment between the lines.

Quick was forever changed by our renegade pageant and its rancorous outcome. Every Christmas after that seemed to have a bittersweet quality. There was the sweetness of the love and unity that came from that incident and the sadness of never knowing what happened to the woman and her baby who had come uninvited to our town and had touched us in such a very special way that we were never quite the same.

Last summer, at a high school reunion, Frankie, Ron, and I were talking about all the crazy things we did when we were students at Quick Junior High. Naturally, the conversation turned to Mary Anne and the baby, and that Christmas.

Ron shook his head as if in disbelief. "You know, I never expected Aunt Harriette to give in so easily."

"She certainly didn't have to," I agreed. "After all, nobody knew . . . ."

Suddenly I caught myself. I had almost betrayed Aunt Harriette's secret. I stammered something like "nobody knew the real Aunt Harriette," but what I was thinking was that she really didn't have to walk off that porch in front of all those people. Her secret was safe. She could have stayed right there. But, and this is what I've come to admire about Aunt Harriette, when she felt the Lord had spoken to her, she did what was right; just like Joseph did when he married Mary.

We stood in silence for a moment, lost in our thoughts.

"I guess there's not a Christmas that goes by that I don't think about Mary Anne," I said.

They looked at me and smiled. "I guess so, 'Daddy,'" Ron said. They laughed. I frowned, trying to hide a smile.

"Me too," said Frankie. "I mean, I always think of her, but lately, you know, I've been thinking about Joshua, too."

"Joshua?" I asked.

"Yeah. You know, he's in his thirties now . . . probably has kids of his own."

What an amazing insight! In his thirties with kids of his own. I still pictured Joshua as a little baby.

"You know what's sad?" Frankie asked. "He never got to know his real mom. And he never got to know how his birth changed our little town."

We were quiet. The conversation seemed a little too serious for adult men.

"I wonder why she named him Joshua," Ron reflected.

"Well," I said, "it's a Hebrew word that means 'Yahweh is salvation.' We're much more familiar with its Greek equivalent – Ya-sous."

"Oh, like the scripture," said Frankie. "'So call him Jesus since he will save people from their sins.' Or something like that."

"Your version is probably closer to the original Greek," Ron said.

"No doubt about it," I added, and then I raised my glass of ginger ale in a toast.

"Gentlemen, a very Merry Christmas to you both," I said.

They laughed and raised their glasses in salute. "And a very Merry Christmas to you, too," they responded.

And it was – at least the memory of a very Merry Christmas – even though this year it came in the middle of August.

O'Tisha Meets the Governor

1 Let every soul be subject unto the higher powers. For there is no power but of God: the powers that be are ordained of God.

2 Whosoever therefore resisteth the power, resisteth the ordinance of God: and they that resist shall receive to themselves damnation.

3 For rulers are not a terror to good works, but to the evil. Wilt thou then not be afraid of the power? do that which is good, and thou shalt have praise of the same:

4 For he is the minister of God to thee for good. But if thou do that which is evil, be afraid; for he beareth not the sword in vain: for he is the minister of God, a revenger to execute wrath upon him that doeth evil.

Romans 13: 1 - 4
King James Version

To my knowledge, my grandmother, O'Tisha Skeens Smith, never darkened a voting booth in the eighty-nine years that she lived on this earth. However, she read the daily newspaper from cover to cover, assiduously watched all of the news programs on TV, and provided a political commentary on what was wrong with American politicians to anyone who would listen. Being isolated on a farm in the hills of West Virginia did not keep her from having strong opinions when it came to how government – local, state, national and international – should be run.

Had "Tish" voted, I can assure you that she would always have voted for "the right man." I can also assure you that the "right man" would always have been a Democrat. By virtue of political party selection, Republicans were automatically disqualified as "right men."

Once, during the 1950's, the barnyard cat brushed against Ole Bossie, frightening the poor cow and causing her to make a sudden and unexpected maneuver that knocked over the milk pail and bruised Grandma's foot. Like any red-blooded American, my Grandmother searched her repertoire for just the right expletive for the devil cat. Her choice was to call the cat a "Damned Old Eisenhower."

In the living room of my grandparent's small farm house were two pictures. One was an oval picture of three women standing at the scenic overlook at Hawk's Nest, West Virginia. I never knew for sure who the three women were.

The other picture was of Franklin Delano Roosevelt, and it had decorated the same place on the wall since he was elected president in 1933.

When my grandmother died of a stroke at the age of eighty-nine, she was sitting in a chair just across the room from that picture. It comforts me to think that, in her dying moment, she found strength to cross the River Styx in the face of the smiling president.

My grandfather's legs had been badly burned in an industrial accident in the early 1920's, and he was disabled. However, his disabilities did not keep him from daylight to dark farm chores, but they slowed him down some and he would occasionally have to be treated at a hospital in Charleston, West Virginia.

It was one such occasion that my whole family made a pilgrimage to the hospital to see Grandpa. Dad and Mom crowded five kids ranging in age from two to twelve, themselves, and Grandma Tish into a 1949 Hudson sedan, and off we went.

It was a week day and my dad was on vacation, so we decided to do some sightseeing after visiting Grandpa. At least that's what I thought when we stopped at the West Virginia State Capitol building in Charleston. The truth was that dad had some business to conduct at the Department of Motor Vehicles, so we toured the building while we waited for him. Then, as now, it was a long wait.

For us kids, however, it was an immense enjoyment to walk (or run) through the rotunda of the Capitol building, talking loudly and stomping our feet so we could listen to the echoes. Then, we looked at everything that was to be seen in that part of the Capitol. After that, we went to a museum in one of the wings. My brother, who was ten, assumed the role of tour guide and began directing us around the museum to see old clothing, old furniture, a Mound builder Indian display, and other interesting and uninteresting artifacts.

Along the way, Grandma got tired and wanted to go back and wait at the car. We couldn't wait in the car, because Dad had kept the keys. I'm sure this was a calculated move on his part to keep us kids out of the car.

Grandma was in the early stages of osteoporosis and was already stooped forward noticeably. Over the next few years, her back would bend more and more until she was "bent double." In spite of her condition, she continued to work in the fields and, in fact, had come inside to rest from working in her garden only an hour before she died.

I was chosen to escort Grandma back to the car. I didn't mind. I was getting bored with the museum and Larry's "enlightening" tour.

As we left the museum and started across the rotunda, five men came out of an office and walked across the room toward us. They moved as if they were connected. Slow or fast, left or right, not quite in step, but not quite out of step either.

It was obvious that the man in the middle of the group was the head of this strange ten legged body and everyone moved as he moved. As they came closer, stopping, starting, talking, gesturing, Grandma and I stood and watched in amazement.

Then, just as they were about to pass, the head noticed us. The whole body made a sudden lurching turn and came toward us. We didn't know whether to stand still or run.

When the thing stopped, it reformed into a single line of men with the head in the middle.

"Hello," said the important man. "Are you enjoying your visit?"

Grandma and I looked at each other and nodded, then looked at the man and nodded.

"Good," he said. "And what is your name?" he asked Grandma.

"Tish . . . Tish Smith," she said. He nodded and waited a moment, then turned to me.

"And you?"

"I'm Richie Smith."

"Oh, this is your Grandmother."

We nodded. The man talking to us looked very familiar. I even thought he might be the Governor, but I knew the Governor would never stop and talk with us.

"Where are you from?" he asked.

"Dutch Ridge," Grandma answered.

"Quick," I said at the same time.

"Oh." The man nodded and studied Grandma for a moment. "I know you," he told her. "You're O'Tisha Smith." He was thoughtful for a moment. "O'Tisha," he said to himself. "I've always thought that was such a lovely name," he said to Grandma.

I was now sure that this really was the Governor, but how could he know my Grandma?

"I met your husband once. What's his name? Edgar or Edward."

"Edwin," said my grandmother.

"That's right," announced the Governor. "I met him once. He was checking the mail. We were going to that little cemetery on the knoll by one of your fields."

Grandma was silent, but I'm sure she was wondering the same thing I was. How did the Governor of West Virginia know so much about Edwin and O'Tisha Smith?

"My aunt is Henry Springer's wife," he explained. "Helen Springer is my mother's sister. I used to visit them all the time. But, now, with the demands of government, I don't get out that way much."

He fell silent, reflecting on something past. I wondered how my grandmother was reacting to all of this. This man was not only the Governor of the State of West Virginia. He was a Republican!

"Yes, Aunt Helen has been a great encouragement to me," he said to us and to the others. "She worked in some of my campaigns. In fact, I'd have to say if it weren't for Aunt Helen and Uncle Henry, I wouldn't be Governor of this great state today."

From the corner of my eye, I saw my grandmother wince.

Just then, one of the body parts tugged at the Governor's sleeve. When the Governor turned, the part lifted an arm to show the Governor a watch.

"Oh my. Gotta run. The demands of being Governor."

He stuck his hand out and shook hands with both of us. It was a limp, Republican type of handshake.

"The next time I visit Aunt Helen and Uncle Henry, I'll come around and visit you and Edwin." He turned to me.

"Nice to meet you, Richie," he said. The Governor of West Virginia spoke my name. Boy! Wait till I tell my friends.

Suddenly, the men reformed into their strange little group and off they went, careening across the floor in the same erratic pattern as before. We stood, watching them go, until they disappeared through the large double doors on the far side of the room.

After a moment, Grandma and I turned and left the building. We walked in silence, but I couldn't help wondering what Grandma was thinking. She had met the Governor. He knew her by name, and he knew Grandpa. He's kin to the Springers who live just around the ridge from my grandparents. Surely, she must be impressed, even if he is a Republican. I certainly was.

We found the car and, sure enough, it was locked. So we stood under the shade of a small tree and looked back toward the Capitol. The sky was a wonderful shade of blue and made a perfect backdrop for the gold leaf dome. The sun gleamed and glittered off the light gray stone that formed the rest of the building. As I looked at it, I knew that God must truly love the State of West Virginia to have given us such a beautiful Capitol.

I glanced over at Grandma. She was holding onto the tree and stretching herself, trying to straighten her crooked spine. She too was soaking in the beauty of the sight, enjoying the warmth of the sunshine and the coolness of a gentle breeze. But, I had no idea what was going on inside her mind, until she said, speaking to no one in particular: "I never did like that Helen Springer. And I didn't know why, until now!"

Johnny and the Devil's Assistant

6 Now there was a day when the sons of God came to present themselves before the LORD, and Satan came also among them.

7 And the LORD said unto Satan, Whence comest thou? Then Satan answered the LORD, and said, From going to and fro in the earth, and from walking up and down in it.

8 And the LORD said unto Satan, Hast thou considered my servant Job, that there is none like him in the earth, a perfect and an upright man, one that feareth God, and escheweth evil?

9 Then Satan answered the LORD, and said, Doth Job fear God for nought?

10 Hast not thou made an hedge about him, and about his house, and about all that he hath on every side? thou hast blessed the work of his hands, and his substance is increased in the land.

11 But put forth thine hand now, and touch all that he hath, and he will curse thee to thy face.

12 And the LORD said unto Satan, Behold, all that he hath is in thy power; only upon himself put not forth thine hand. So Satan went forth from the presence of the LORD.

Job 1: 6 - 12
King James Version

MY MOM'S QUITE the world traveler. She goes to Europe about every year to see my brother Larry who teaches in the Department of Defense school for children of service men and women, to Dallas to visit my two sisters who live there, or to Florida to visit her two sisters who live there, and occasionally even to Maryland to visit me and my family as well as her two brothers and mother who live in this area.

Most recently she returned from Florida and we were chatting about how things are going with June and Doris and all the uncles, aunts, cousins, and assorted family friends who have moved to the warmer climate. She was just catching me up on June and John, when she mentioned that Johnny and Jo Johnson had come up to Orlando for a visit from their home in the Tampa area. As mom gave me the latest on Doris and Leslie, thoughts of Johnny Johnson kept tugging at the back of my mind.

Johnny Johnson is the man who undermined one whole facet of my theology. Not that I believe what he says. I don't want you to think that – not for a moment – but there's enough truth in it to make me want to reconsider one of my main tenants, something I've firmly believed in all of my life, and you know how upsetting that can be.

I saw Johnny and Jo about a year ago when I was visiting Mom and Dad. They had come up to West Virginia to see their children who still live in the area. It was a beautiful day and as she prepared the food, my mom suddenly said:

"Let's have a picnic."

"A picnic?" I asked.

"Yeah!" said Jo Johnson. "What a wonderful idea."

"What's this about a picnic?" quizzed Johnny from the living room.

"In your honor," said mom.

"'Mr. Picnic,'" I said. "Isn't that what we called you?"

Johnny laughed.

"Let's see," I continued. "How many picnics a year did we have when you were the Sunday School Superintendent at Quick Church of the Nazarene? It had to be at least six."

"Yeah," said Jo. "The only reason we didn't have *more* was that it gets kind of chilly around here from December through February."

"That didn't stop him," mom added. "Remember, all those indoor picnics we had."

So we got ready to have a picnic – fried chicken, baked beans, potato salad, and all the trimmings. As we were setting up the folding table and chairs in the backyard, I watched Johnny in action. He was a delight as he laughed, joked, and told one story after another. At 69, he's still a bundle of energy and full of life and joy. But my mind went back to a time when that was not the case.

I remember when Johnny and Jo started coming to the Church of the Nazarene in Quick. They just showed up one day – unexpected, but boy were we happy to see them. There was Johnny and Jo and their kids. All of the kid's names started with the letter "J," there were seven of them, and the oldest was about eleven. Sunday School attendance at the church nearly doubled.

It didn't take long for Johnny and Jo to become a very important part of our church. Everyone liked Johnny, adults and kids alike. He took a special interest in all the young people. He made sure there were always a lot of activities for us and took us on special outings.

He was even instrumental in the purchase of the 1946 Ford school bus that served as our church bus. My dad, who was a non-attender, but who was a mechanic at a Ford garage in Charleston, spent many hours working on that old bus to get it running. I'm sure it was less than a "spiritual experience" for

Dad, and in fact may have been a fundamental contributor to his apostasy.

But in those days, there was something a little "peculiar" about Johnny; a basic instability.

When he was up, he was very, very up. But when he was down, he was horrid. It would happen about every four or five weeks. Jo and the kids would show up for church, but no Johnny. When someone asked Jo about him, she'd just shrug, look kind of sad, and say: "Oh, he's having a big fight with the Devil," then change the subject.

These "fights with the Devil" really knocked the wind out of Johnny. When the bout was over, he'd stand up in testimony meeting, weep, and talk about how difficult it was and how he had to pray and fast to make it through. Then he'd give us a lecture on how we should live pure lives and not give the Devil a foothold.

Johnny was always optimistic after these bouts. He'd say that he felt that he'd finally conquered the Devil. He seemed more cheerful than ever and went out of his way to make up for things that didn't get done while he was going through his trials. Then, in about a month or so, Jo and the kids would arrive for church without Johnny.

I vividly remember the time when all of us, including Johnny, thought the Devil was going to be the winner and that we'd lose Johnny forever.

Everyone figured that it was "business as usual" the first Sunday Jo and the kids showed up without Johnny. But when he didn't show up the second Sunday, people started to become concerned. There was some whispering and a lot more prayers for Johnny.

By the third Sunday, concern became alarm. There were those serious whispered conversations not meant for children to hear in which Johnny's name was mentioned. The pastor made two or three trips to see Johnny the next week, there were a lot of phone call conversations with very concerned voices, and we were just about all sure that Johnny Johnson was losing this bout with the Devil.

The fourth Sunday morning came and went – no Johnny. Then Sunday night, there he was. He was all smiles and jokes, but to look at him, you know that Johnny was not the same man that he had been three weeks earlier. He looked haggard and worn. You could tell that this latest battle had been an immense struggle, but you could also see that Johnny Johnson was different. He had won and won big.

Johnny didn't say much that night. He cried a lot, hugged everyone, shook a lot of hands, and told people how much he loved and appreciated them. We wanted to know about his fight with the Devil. We knew it must have been quite a battle and we wanted to hear about it. But nothing was said. We even sang Johnny's favorite song: Glorious Freedom – with a verse that said: "Once I was bound by Sin's rolling fetters, chained like a slave I struggled in vain, but I received a glorious freedom when

Jesus rent those fetters in twain." But Johnny still wasn't talking.

Wednesday night at Quick Church of the Nazarene was "prayer meeting." It was a time for songs, testimonies, a "short" sermon, and an old-time congregational prayer. For prayer, we all knelt, either at our chairs or up front at the altar, and we all prayed out loud at the same time. We thought this would be the night Johnny would tell about his latest battle with the Devil, so we were all there. Some who might have felt the need to study for a test the next day or to catch up on homework, or who may not have been feeling well, were all there anyway – just in case Johnny talked. We weren't disappointed.

After a few songs, the announcements, and some other preliminary activities, Johnny was the first on his feet. He spoke with a special calmness in his voice, and here's what he told us:

"I've been through a really difficult time over the past several weeks, and I want to thank all those who prayed for me and called me and came by, and I want to thank everyone who was concerned. As you know, I have had a lot of battles with the Devil over the last year or so, and some of these battles were so real that I could actually smell the burning sulfur from the fires of hell.

"During these times, I wasn't so much tempted to return to a life of sin as I was just to give up. I really wasn't much of a sinner to begin with. I didn't do a lot of the things we associate with sin like drinking and smoking and carousing, so there wasn't any temptation to do those things since I never did them in the first place. There were just all these doubts, all these feelings of inadequacy – that I'm not a good Christian and never will be, that I'm not a good friend or a good father or a good husband and that I'm not capable of being any of these things. And when I'd got to thinking about these things, I'd just go into some kind of really deep depression and think I'd never get out. I was too tired to sleep, too tired to think – just very, very weary.

"First of all, I'd have trouble getting to sleep and when I finally did, I'd wake up at two or three in the morning and not be able to go back to sleep. I was miserable. Then last Sunday morning, after Jo and the kids left for church, I walked the floor and prayed for deliverance. But it felt as if the heavens were brass. I just felt exhausted and I went in and got into bed. After a while I went to sleep.

"Then I began to have this dream. It was an awful dream. If it had been night, it would have been called a nightmare, so I guess I was having a 'daymare.'"

We laughed. Johnny was true to form.

"I dreamed that someone had me by the arm and was dragging me along a path of some sort. It was dark, but there seemed to be some small amount of light and I thought it must be the Devil who had hold of me, but I couldn't see.

Then we came out into an open area and *there* was the Devil. We were near a cliff and beyond the cliff it was totally black. I don't know why, but for some reason I knew that we were standing on the edge of outer darkness and I was about to be cast into it.

"But what puzzled me most was who had hold of me. I tried to see, but my dream was very confused. For some reason, I felt I knew the person but I couldn't figure out who it was. Suddenly, the Devil pointed toward the edge of the cliff and said 'cast him into outer darkness where there will be weeping and wailing and gnashing of teeth.' And that's when I heard this mournful sound coming from beyond the cliff. It sounded like the cries of people in terrible agony. Then this person, this 'Devil's Assistant,' began dragging me toward the edge of the cliff. I tried to cry out, but there was no sound. I tried to fight off the Devil's Assistant, but he had a strong grip on me. I tried to see who it was and when I finally got a glimpse of him I could see he had a black hood over his face. I kept feeling like I knew him, but I couldn't see him. Closer we came to the edge. I cried, I fought, but it was all to no avail. Then, when I was right on the edge, I grabbed hold of the hood and yanked. Just as I did, the Devil's Assistant gave me a push and I went sailing backwards out into the darkness, screaming at the top of my lungs. But I had caught a glimpse of him, just enough that I knew who he was.

"I guess it was the scream that woke me. I sat straight up in the bed. My mouth was dry as cotton. I looked at my hand, and I was holding the pillow case that I had pulled off one of the pillows. Then I looked up, and there, staring me in the face was the Devil's Assistant. We looked at each other for a moment, and then I fell backward onto the bed, exhausted and very disappointed. You see, what had happened is that when I sat up I was staring into the mirror on the dresser and I knew that the face staring back at me from that mirror was the same as the one under the hood. I had met the Devil's Assistant, and he was me.

"Well, I lay there for quite a while, thinking about what all this meant. I knew it was true. I knew that all the doubts and fears were really my own and that I was really the source of my own defeat.

"The next thing I did was to look up every passage in the Bible that referred to the Devil or to Satan or to demons and I made some amazing discoveries. For one thing, the Devil is not nearly as powerful as we make him out to be. We sometimes think he's as powerful as God, but he's not. For another thing, we give credit to the Devil for a lot of things he doesn't do. He doesn't need to do them. He's got us to do them for him. We blame a lot of things on the Devil that are really the responsibility of the Devil's Assistant – namely me or you!"

Johnny Johnson stood quietly for several very silent seconds before he spoke next: "I'll tell you one thing you can bank on, and I hope you'll join me in this. I promise you that I will never be the Devil's Assistant again. Paul says that we are to resist the Devil and he will flee from us. Well, I'm more than resisting. I will never be party to my own defeat at the hands of the Devil, or anyone else for that matter."

Johnny sat down. We all sat there in silence. What could we say? Johnny had certainly said it all. I looked around. I was sure that there were some people there who might have been a little uncomfortable about some of the things Johnny had said. I'm sure that there were those who may not have wanted their children to hear that part about giving the Devil credit for things he doesn't do, or that part about us being responsible for a lot of things that the Devil gets blamed for.

But I'll say this about Johnny – he kept his promise. His battles with the Devil were through. He became more cheerful than ever and just never seemed to be unhappy or depressed about anything, even when he was sick. He was always there with a kind word or a smile or a joke to cheer you up. And he never missed another worship service to do battle with the Devil again. In fact, I never heard him say much at all about the Devil after that. He seemed to "grow stronger in the Lord," as Aunt Harriette would say, and within a year he was our Sunday School Superintendent and a very important person to our church.

As for me, I thought about what Johnny said for a long time. In fact, for quite a while, every time I looked in a mirror I couldn't help but wonder if I was looking into the face of the Devil's Assistant.

And I began to listen to what other people said about the Devil, how they perceived the Devil and their responsibility for their own actions, and there were times when I thought that maybe, just maybe, Johnny might have been right. I'm not saying he was – just *maybe* he was!

Well, what Johnny said that night in Prayer Meeting was ultraorthodox theology compared to what he said to me in a private conversation three or four years later. It was the summer before I went to Trevecca Nazarene College. He and I were doing some fix-up work on the church one Saturday afternoon. We were chitchatting about a lot of things, and I mentioned how much his testimony about his battles with the Devil had made a strong impression on me and had helped me take the responsibility for some feelings and actions that I might otherwise have blamed on the Devil.

Johnny seemed surprised that I even remembered the story. He looked at me for a long minute. I felt uncomfortable, as if I had mentioned an awful secret that had been buried away in his subconscious and had now been brought out into the open. He looked around, as if to see if anyone else were present. Suddenly, I got the feeling that he was about to confess to me some very deep dark secret, something he'd never revealed to anyone before. And I was right.

"I personally don't believe in the Devil," he said.

I was stunned at this heresy coming from our own Sunday School Superintendent, but I tried not to show it. This was an admission of something very fundamental to our religious life and I didn't want to embarrass Johnny in any way. And besides, I didn't know what he might do.

"You what?" I said. But I sort of whispered it loudly. Johnny stepped a little closer and whispered back.

"I myself . . . I personally don't believe in the Devil."

"But Johnny," I whispered, "you're a Nazarene. Nazarenes *have* to believe in the Devil."

"No we don't! I checked. There's nothing in the Manual that says that believing in the Devil is a requirement for membership. The Trinity, yes. But not the Devil."

"I can't believe that!"

"It's true. Look it up."

I didn't know what to say. It was bad enough to find out that Johnny, a man I held in great esteem, did not believe in the Devil, but to find out that it was not a requirement for membership in the church of which I'd been a member since I was old enough to be eligible for membership was a double blow.

"But . . . but, what about the Bible. The Bible talks about the Devil. How can you say that there's no Devil?"

"I'm not saying there is no Devil."

"So, you're saying there is a Devil?"

"No, I'm not saying that either."

"Well, what are you saying?"

"If you'd listen, I'll tell you!"

"All right, I'm listening."

"What I'm saying is that to me, personally, the Devil doesn't exist."

"But you just said that you weren't saying he doesn't exist."

"Richie, just listen to me. Read my lips. To me . . . ." He pointed at his chest. "To me, myself, and I, personally, I live my life as though there is no Devil."

"But there is. Right?"

"You're missing the point. It doesn't matter if there is a Devil or not. It's all in how people perceive him. Some people think he's as powerful as God. To those people he's an overwhelming force and they live defeated lives and blame it all on the Devil. Just like I did. Know what I mean?"

I was a little reluctant to admit it: "Well, let's say that I'm aware that some people overemphasize the Devil's power."

"And there are other people who think the Devil is a fallen angel who is the leader of the dark forces, but that he's not as powerful as God and as a result, they aren't always being dragged down by this overpowering force. Right?"

"Okay. Maybe you're right about that."

"Well, instead of believing that the Devil is powerful or not powerful, I choose to believe he doesn't exist!"

He was beginning to make sense and that worried me. "But, just because *you* don't believe in him doesn't mean he's not out there!"

"As far as I'm concerned it does."

"Johnny, I . . . ." I was in a pickle. What he was saying sort of made sense if you understand it as a personal thing and don't take it too literally. Besides I was running out of rational arguments. So I decided to bring in the big guns.

"What would Aunt Harriette and the preacher say if they knew you didn't believe in the Devil?" I asked. But he knew I was teasing.

"Oh, I imagine that they'd say I've been tricked by the Devil into believing that he doesn't exist."

"Right. And you know Aunt Harriette. She certainly believes in the Devil."

We stood smiling at each other for a few moments. Then Johnny became very serious.

"Think about it," he said. "The Devil is only as powerful as you let him be. And in my case, he has absolutely no power at all, because as far as I'm concerned, he doesn't exist."

Now, here we were, several years later, having a picnic in Johnny's honor. And there he was, the ever-buoyant personality, the man who had given up his job as the Devil's Assistant, and in the process had lost his belief in a Devil. And, if that wasn't bad enough, he'd infected me with his heresy!

The dinner was over. We folded the table and chairs and put them away. Then Mom and Jo began washing dishes and cleaning up the kitchen. Dad decided to walk down the drive to the main road to get the mail and the newspaper. It was his way of walking off all the food he had eaten. Johnny and I chose instead to settle in overstuffed deck chairs on the big back porch. We nursed hot coffee and made insincere offers to help clean up.

Our conversation turned to some news event of the day; I don't even remember what it was now, and Mom, as she "warmed up our coffee" and headed back into the house, made her pronouncement about the matter.

"It's all the work of the Devil," she said.

Johnny sat staring into his cup until Mom was inside the house. Then he looked at me and smiled. I knew that I was about to get the next installment in Johnny Johnson's "The Devil doesn't exist" theology. I couldn't wait. But I also couldn't let this pass without getting in a little "dig."

"Maybe we should ask Mom to come back out so you can explain the error of her ways," I teased.

He smiled broadly. "Reality is as it's perceived to be."

"Well, now that you've totally destroyed my faith in a Devil . . . ."

"Did I?" he asked. "I hope so. Because if I did, I may have saved you from yourself."

"As I was saying, since you've destroyed my faith in the Devil, why don't you catch me up on your latest thinking about the subject. I'm sure you've been giving it some consideration since our last conversation about the matter."

"You're right about that! When did we have that conversation?"

"It's not necessary for us to pursue injurious questions related to the aging process."

"Right. Anyway, I really took a chance telling you what I was thinking . . . my . . . what would you call it? 'Un-theology?'"

"De-ology?"

"Close enough. Well, I was worried about it at first . . . ."

"Afraid I'd tell Aunt Harriette?"

"A little, I guess." He looked at me sternly. "Will you stop interrupting and let me tell this?"

"Just playing a hunch."

"Well, after a while I decided it was a good thing that I told you. It was the first time I had said it out loud and it helped me. Plus, your comments helped me focus on what I actually believed."

"So, have you come back into the fold?"

"Quite the contrary. I now believe what I believe more firmly than ever."

"Which is?"

"Well, you know, I never really ever said that there is no Devil."

"Okay. I'll buy that. It just sounded like that's what you were saying."

"When you read the Bible," he continued, ignoring my interruption, "there's a lot said about the Devil. You know, the Book of Job, which some people say is one of the oldest books in the Bible, talks about the Devil, so it's a concept that goes way back. It's basically a belief that there is some kind of adversary who is greater than ourselves and that this person is the source of a lot of our problems, both physically and spiritually.

"In the case of Job, Satan tempts God to take away his wall of protection and let Job really have it. God agrees, and that's the last we hear about the Devil."

"Hmm. I never thought of that."

"It's true. Job doesn't blame Satan for his problems."

"He blames God."

"Right. But that's a whole 'nother theological question that we don't have time to deal with right now."

Johnny stopped to think for a moment, and then continued. "Some people say that Job is fiction. That it's an early form of drama or literature that intended to deal with the problem of pain and suffering – why good people suffer. I don't know if I'm ready to buy the fiction part just yet. I guess, as far as I'm concerned, it doesn't really matter if Job is a real person or not. The issue of suffering is still very real."

"But, if it's fiction, it means we can take the mention of Satan less seriously."

"No. Not really. Well, yes. Maybe."

"That's what I like, decisiveness!"

He ignored me. "Job's a minor consideration. Let's look at the Book of Revelation."

"A great book for De-ologists."

"My thoughts exactly. Plus you have the writings of Paul who not only talks about a Devil, but an underworld full of sub-devils, and that we're at war with all these creatures."

"So, what's all this mean?"

"Well, as far as I'm concerned, it means that if you want to believe in the Devil, you certainly have a lot of scriptural proof."

"And that if you choose not to believe in the Devil, you don't have a leg to stand on."

"More or less. But the point is, how do you perceive the Devil?"

"And how *do* you perceive the Devil?"

"As far as I'm concerned, he doesn't exist!"

I heard a noise. I looked up. It was startling to think that my mother might suddenly round the corner and overhear this man she had respected all of her life saying such blasphemous things about the Devil. It was just a bird helping itself to some leftover crumbs.

"How can you say that in light of what you just said about the Bible?" I asked.

"You remember a few years ago when some theologians were saying that God was dead?"

"Do I remember it? I was in Grad School at the time and heard a lot of good logical expositions on why those guys were going to burn in hell."

"Well, there was one guy, down in Atlanta, I think. And I don't know if he said it or if someone said that they thought that even though he didn't say it, it was what he meant to say."

"Sounds reasonable, either way."

"Anyway, what was said – or what was meant – was that God was really not *dead*, but that we have to live in the world *as if* God is dead."

"I remember something about that."

"Well, when I read that, I thought 'that's what I believe.'"

"That we have to live as though God is dead?"

"No! Will you stop that? I thought that's what I believe about the Devil. I live in the world as though God is alive and as though the Devil is dead."

"The Devil is Dead De-ology. Certainly is a catchy title."

"I like it. And I like the concept. To me, the Devil is dead."

"Don't tell Mom."

"Is she the new Aunt Harriette?"

"No, not really, but she puts a lot of faith in the works of the Devil."

Johnny was quiet for a moment. "Here's something else to think about. You know all that stuff about the Devil being an angel and rebelling against God and falling from heaven and setting up an opposing government of a sort that is trying to usurp God."

"Yep. It's an important part of our Deology."

"It never happened."

"It what?"

"Well, let me back up and say it this way. It's not in the Bible."

I was stunned. I was sure it was somewhere in the Bible. After all, I was a graduate of a theological seminary. I should know.

"Are you sure?"

"Find it."

I thought about it for a while. "What about that passage in Isaiah about Lucifer?"

"I knew you'd say that. Do you know what the word 'Lucifer' means?"

"I'm sure I'm about to find out."

"It's the name the Hebrews gave to the Morning Star. And that passage is not talking about a fallen angel at all, but a fallen national or international leader. If someone hadn't already told you that Lucifer is supposed to be the Devil and that he rebelled against God and fell from heaven, you'd never get it from that passage."

"Sort of like, making up the theory, and then looking for any evidence that might support it."

"Right."

"You've thought this thing through pretty well, haven't you?"

"Well, I guess I decided what I believe a long time ago and I've spent the last thirty plus years looking for any evidence that might support it."

"At least you're honest."

He smiled, but it was sort of a sad smile.

"No, I'm not. If I was honest, I'd tell people that I don't believe there's a Devil. But I can't. I can hint at it, I can tell them that he's not all that powerful, that if they just resist him he'll flee, I can tell them not to give up so easily. I can't even tell Jo what I believe. I'm just not sure that she would understand. You're the only person that I've ever told."

"I don't know if I'm honored or not."

"Well, at least you're not out looking for a stake and gathering firewood."

"Oh, we're civilized. First we do the wood splints under the fingernails to see if you'll recant."

"I only know what I experienced, all the hell I went through, and I know it wasn't the Devil, it was me. That much I know for sure."

He paused a moment, thinking, then continued:

"I'll tell you what bothers me the most: that people are living in defeat and despair because they think that there's some supernatural demon out there who's trying to ruin their lives, or that they are refusing to accept responsibility for their actions because they can justify copping-out on what they did by saying that some cosmic bad guy made them do it."

"But people need the Devil, don't they? They need to be able to personify evil so that they are struggling against a person not some intangible force; they need to feel that someone more powerful than themselves is leading them astray, and they need to have someone to blame for the things they do that are wrong."

"You're right. And they have all the biblical evidence to support the existence of this sub-supreme being. Plus, they have a lot of myths like that stuff about the fallen angel."

"So, we're agreed then. There really is a somewhat powerful personal being who personifies evil, who entices us to sin, and who deserves all the blame we can give him."

"As I said: 'Reality is as we perceive it to be.'"

"In other words, I can believe anything I want, but as far as *you're* concerned, the Devil is dead."

"Absolutely!"

"You two going to sit out here all day?" It was Jo.

"Well, we were just thinking about trying to find out where the dessert is."

She came over and stood next us. "Would you look at that! I can't take you anywhere. You spilled baked beans on your brand-new shirt!"

He looked down at the small stain about halfway down the shirt. Then he looked up at Jo. "The Devil made me do it," he announced.

"Humph! I don't believe that for a moment." She started back toward the house. Johnny looked at me and smiled.

"Well, maybe I'm making some headway after all!"

After bidding goodbye to mom and dad and hanging up the phone, I spent a little time reflecting on Johnny Johnson, formerly the Devil's Assistant and now the main proponent of the "Devil Is Dead De-ology." Please don't think that because I lend a sympathetic ear to Johnny that I accept the theories that he espouses. They do have a certain appeal, but I'm one of those who needs the Devil. I'm just not ready yet to start accepting the responsibility for my own actions. I mean, think about it. What if everyone thought the way Johnny Johnson does. Why, we'd be in a devil of a fix.

Lefty

13 And Moses said unto God, Behold, when I come unto the children of Israel, and shall say unto them, The God of your fathers hath sent me unto you; and they shall say to me, What is his name? what shall I say unto them?

14 And God said unto Moses, I AM THAT I AM: and he said, Thus shalt thou say unto the children of Israel, I AM hath sent me unto you.

Exodus 3:13 - 14
King James Version

WE CALLED HIM LEFTY because of a birth defect that caused him to lead with his left shoulder when he walked. Actually, there was some debate as to whether it was a birth defect or something that might have happened to him soon after he was born. His parents always claimed that he was born that way, but there were others who saw him not long after his birth and claimed that he was normal at first.

Aunt Harriette would have known since she was the midwife for his birth, but you could never get her to say. I never talked to her about it myself, but when others asked, her only response was that he was born healthy and that we should be thankful for that.

Anyway, he walked crooked and his face looked like someone had squeezed it in a vice.

Because of his looks, Lefty was very shy. Some people took his shyness as being "slow," but he was just shy and that was because he didn't feel comfortable when he was around other people. When people came to visit, he slipped away to his room. And when the teachers asked questions of the class at school, he wouldn't speak up even when he knew the answer because he didn't want the other kids to look at him.

No, Lefty was not slow. In fact, he was the opposite. He may not have been a genius like my cousin Morris Morris, but he was an avid reader and, in fact, was given a double promotion from the second grade to the fourth.

I liked Lefty and we got along fine even though he was three years older than me. When we went to visit his family and he'd sneaked off to his room, I'd slip up to see him. He would always be reading a book – his room was full of them – and he'd tell me wonderful stories and interesting facts. He would also help me with my school work. I aced a couple of tests because he told me what questions to study for. He had taken the same test a couple of years before and it was like he had memorized all the questions or something.

If no one else was visiting but me and Mom, Lefty wouldn't hide in his room. Instead, the two of us would go for long walks in the woods and he'd tell me lots of things about nature. He knew every tree by bark and leaf, and all the birds by their songs, and stuff like that.

There was a large rock outcropping about a mile from their house and that was a favorite spot for us. It was on the point of the ridge and we would sit on the edge of a very large rock, looking down about a hundred feet onto the treetops below. It was quite a sight.

When televisions started appearing in homes in the mid-1950's, Lefty was fascinated. After seeing one on display at a store in Charleston, he read everything he could get his hands on about cathode ray tubes and electronic circuitry and could explain in detail just how television worked, tracing light waves from the studio, into the camera, through the tubes and wires and into the airwaves until they came out of a home television set.

Even though he was fascinated by the internal workings of the television, he was even more captivated to see the picture. He would sit in stunned silence before the set, delight dancing in his eyes as he watched. You could have dropped the atomic bomb in the living room and he'd never have noticed.

What delighted him most were the cartoons, the love of which we both shared. In fact, he liked cartoons so much that he dared venture from the safety of his home and make the trip to our house in Quick, a three-mile walk, to watch cartoons with me.

We were one of the first families in Quick to have a TV and since he felt comfortable with me he'd come to our house for a couple of hours and we'd watch cartoons on Saturday mornings. My brother and sisters soon came to be comfortable with Lefty, so it was a treat for him to be seen and accepted by other kids.

When he was in high school, Lefty became interested in the Mystery Religions that flourished in the Roman Empire around the time of Christ. Although Lefty seldom attended church, he read the Bible and could quote scripture better than most of our preachers. He also read current and past theologians and books by ancient writers like Augustine and Thomas Aquinas. But it was the Mystery Religions that fascinated Lefty most.

"They weren't really a mystery like we think of a mystery," he told me. "They were only a mystery to the outsiders. It's like the Book of Revelation. The Christians at the end of the first century read and understood it perfectly, but to the Romans, it was just a bunch of nonsense."

"Sort of like it is to people today?" I asked.

"Yes," he said. "But I wouldn't say that in front of too many people. You know what happened to Joan of Arc."

"Yeah. Sort of," I said. I decided I should look up Joan of Arc in the encyclopedia at school to see what really happened to her and thus what might also happen to me. After reading about her, I decided not to make that comment about the Book of Revelation again.

Lefty and I decided to have our own Mystery Religion. We came up with a secret handshake and some code words which only we knew the meaning of. Our secret meeting place was the rock cliff. Sometimes when we were having dinner with his family, he'd say something to me in our secret code language that meant that we'd meet later at the rock. Then he'd go one way and I'd go another and we'd meet there.

It was kind of fun, but we didn't have any secret rituals or other things so our mystery religion would probably have died out completely if it hadn't been for the cartoons – actually, one cartoon: Popeye.

Our favorite cartoons were Warner Bros. cartoons. He liked Bugs Bunny while I favored Daffy Duck. We both laughed a lot at the Road Runner cartoon, but we always rooted for the Wile E. Coyote. I think it had something to do with being the underdog.

One Saturday morning I noticed that Lefty had his focus firmly fixed on the Popeye cartoons. And he wasn't laughing. He seemed to be studying them for some reason. The next week the same thing happened. In fact, he got upset if I laughed too loud or asked him something during one of the Popeye cartoons.

The following week, after watching a Popeye cartoon in silence, he turned to me and announced: "I think I've discovered something very significant."

"What?"

"Can't tell you now," he said. "It's a mystery."

The way he said "mystery," I knew something was up and that I'd have to wait until our next secret meeting at the rock cliff to find out.

"Okay," he said in a whisper as we nestled on the rock precipice. "Here's what I think." He hesitated and looked around as if to make sure no one was hiding behind a bush, listening to our conversation. "Popeye is a mystery religion."

"What?"

"Yeah. I'm sure of it."

"How?"

"Well," he said, and took a deep breath, "when Moses was in the desert talking to the burning bush which was really God, what did God say His name was?"

"Moses' name?"

"No! What did God say that His name was . . . God's name."

"I don't remember."

"Think about it. Moses said 'who will I say has sent me?' Remember that?"

"Yeah."

"And what did God say?"

"Tell them . . . tell them that 'I hath sent you?' No, wait. 'I am hath sent you.' Something like that."

"Yes, but just before that God said to Moses "I am that I am.""

"Yeah. I remember that."

"Okay. And who does Popeye say that he is?"

I thought about it. "Popeye?"

"The song Sing the song."

"Let's see. 'I'm Popeye the sailor man. I sleep in a garbage can . . . .'"

"Not that version."

"Oh. Let me think. 'I am what I am and that's all what . . . I . . . am.' Oh."

"See!"

"You think Popeye is God?"

"No. It's a mystery religion. The mystery or the secret is that Popeye *represents* God."

"That's dumb."

"Don't be too quick to jump to conclusions. Let's look at it some more."

"Okay, but I still think . . . ."

"What about Bluto? Who does he represent?"

"Bluto?"

"Yeah. Think about it."

"The Devil!" I exclaimed.

"Shh! You're right. But not so loud."

"It's just a coincidence."

"Is it? There's more."

"Like what?"

"Spinach."

"Spinach represents something?"

"Think about it. What does the spinach give Popeye?"

"Strength?"

"Right, but take it a little further."

I thought a moment. "Power!" I said. I was awe struck. "The Holy Spirit," I whispered in reverence.

"Right. And isn't there always a whirlwind motion associated with Popeye's arm or his pipe when he eats the spinach?"

"Like a rushing mighty wind," I quoted from the Book of Acts.

"You got it."

We were silent for a few moments. Lefty seemed to be studying the tops of the trees below us. I waited. Finally I turned to him and asked: "Who else?"

"Olive Oyl," he said in a very matter-of-fact manner.

"Olive Oyl? Who is *she*?"

"Not 'who *is* she?' Who does she *represent*. It's a mystery religion, remember."

"Oh, right. Okay who does she represent?"

"Who would you think?"

I thought. "Olive Oyl. Olive Oyl. Uh . . . Mary?" It was just a wild guess.

"So you see it too."

"I'm right?"

"Absolutely. And you know what sealed it for me?"

"What?"

"I went shopping with mom. We were in the cooking oil section and I saw this bottle of olive oil. I went over and looked at it and you know what it said on the label?"

"What?"

"Virgin."

"Really?"

"Really."

I thought about Olive Oyl a moment. "Of course, she could represent the Church," I told Lefty.

"The Bride of Christ! I hadn't thought of that."

I felt pleased. "So," I ventured, "if we say that Olive Oyl is . . . I mean, represents Mary, does that mean Sweet Pea is . . . ?" I couldn't bring myself to say it.

"The baby Jesus?"

"Yes."

"Well, technically Olive Oyl is not Sweet Pea's mother."

"Oh." I was disappointed.

"But, it's the nature of a mystery religion to use such figures even when there's no literal connection."

"So, it could be that Sweet Pea represents the baby Jesus?"

"There are other associations that make that possible," he said. "While Sweet Pea's mother was mentioned in one episode, I've never seen a reference to his father."

"Whoa. You mean, like it could be like the virgin birth?"

"I think it is very likely the case."

"What about those three kids who are always causing problems for Popeye? Aren't they cousins or something?"

"Peter, James, and John."

"Is that really their names?"

"No! That's who they represent."

"Or the Trinity."

"I thought of that too, but I don't think so."

"Why not?" I asked.

"They're too human. And, like you said, they're always getting into trouble and needing to be rescued by Popeye."

"I see your point."

"Besides, the real Peter, James, and John may have been related."

"Cousins?" I asked in almost a whisper.

"Cousins," he said.

I thought about the other characters in the cartoons. "Who do you think Wimpy is?" I asked.

Lefty was thoughtful for a moment. "Wimpy doesn't represent one person," he said. "I think Wimpy represents a class of people."

"Who?"

"Mankind."

"Makes sense."

"Yes it does. Wimpy is, well, wimpy. He's just like a lot of people. He's always trying to bum money which he will never pay back even though he promises he will. And he's always hungry."

"I can see the resemblance," I said.

We sat in silence for several minutes, bathing in the sun and staring out over the valley.

"So, what do we do now?" I asked.

"Nothing. That's the whole purpose of a mystery religion. We know the secret, so we're on the inside."

"And," I added, "when we watch Popeye cartoons we'll learn more and see even greater connections."

"Right! But as for now, we just keep this to ourselves."

"Does this mean we shouldn't laugh when we see a Popeye cartoon?"

"No. No. We have to laugh. Otherwise, people might get suspicious."

"Good point," I said.

"But it does mean that we'll never watch a Popeye cartoon the same ever again. Knowing the mystery has changed our lives forever."

As it turned out that was one of the Prophet of Popeyeology's prophecies that came true.

Mary Margaret Mahoney

46 Then there arose a reasoning among them, which of them should be greatest.

47 And Jesus, perceiving the thought of their heart, took a child, and set him by him,

48 And said unto them, Whosoever shall receive this child in my name receiveth me: and whosoever shall receive me receiveth him that sent me: for he that is least among you all, the same shall be great.

Luke 9: 46 - 48
King James Version

DURING OUR SOJOURN from the mountains of West Virginia, some members of my family, including myself, settled near Washington, D.C. So, once or twice a year, Mom and Dad would make the trip up the "Northern Route," through Morgantown, and down into Maryland to visit. While they were here, we would always get together with the rest of the family who live in the area.

The "Virginia Kennedys" include Mom's mother, Edith, and two of Mom's brothers, Dave and Ron and their families.

It was a Saturday afternoon when we made the pilgrimage to Virginia to visit the family and to see Dave and Kay's new townhouse. My dad always talks about selling the old homestead and moving someplace that doesn't require extensive upkeep. This "upkeep" consists mostly of lawn mowing. And it's not that the yard is so large. In fact, it isn't very large at all. The mitigating factor is that much of the yard is at about a sixty-degree incline.

But once he saw the townhouse – how close the neighbors were, how small the parking lots are, and how little overall privacy he would have compared to living up the hollow near Quick, talk of buying such a place quickly passed from the scene.

We were having a good time visiting the family. Dave and Kay's kids and grandkids were there. Ron and Carol and their kids and grandkids were there. Grandma Edith was there. My daughter and her family were there. Aunt Kay's sister and her husband were there. All in all there must have been 25 to 30 of us.

When the family gets together like this, we often sit around in a large group and talk about the "old days." These are not necessarily the "good old days," however. The group discussions are times of great enjoyment, but also times of anxiety. We know too many embarrassing stories about each other – stories about the incredibly stupid things we did when we were growing up. So, when we're together in a group, there's an uneasy sort of truce – a kind of balance of power that says "if you don't tell your story about me, I won't tell my story about you."

We all know that one little "remembrance" could bring the whole thing crashing down and the battle to see who could tell the most outrageous story would begin. When we get started with these stories, it's not a pretty sight. There is a lot of laughter, however. Some at my expense. I've learned not to defend myself against these on-sloughs. I just sit there grinning and plotting my revenge.

But this particular day, I was relaxed. Since we were such a large group, we had resorted to our small group mode in which we "bunch-up" into groups of five to ten people and talk about whatever interests us. (Mostly we talk about what each of us has been doing for the past six months or so since the last get-together.)

I was with one group – mostly men, but I was eavesdropping on another group whose conversation I found to be a little more interesting.

I was listening to someone telling a story. I believe it was my Aunt Kay. She grew up just over the ridge from Quick, so we knew a lot of the same people. I was really only half listening, but when she said the name Mary Margaret Mahoney the strangest thing happened.

Well, actually, a couple of strange things happened, but one caused me quite a bit more concern than the other.

The first thing that happened, the one of lesser concern, was that I lost track of what the people in my group were saying. That would not have been so critical, but it happened just as someone asked me a question. All of a sudden I noticed that everyone was looking at me, waiting for an answer.

To make matters worse, the other thing that was going on in my mind, the thing that had caused me so much concern, took me by such a surprise that I couldn't make a quick recovery. (Actually I couldn't make a recovery at all.). There we sat: they staring at me and me staring back.

My uncle Ron tried to prompt me by saying "Well?" But that only made matters worse and I blurted out what I was thinking. I said "Mary Margaret Mahoney." Since they had not overheard the other group's conversation, they had no idea what I was talking about and why I said her name.

Instead they connected her name to the question that had been asked, and, although to this day I don't know what the question was, evidently "Mary Margaret Mahoney" was not only the wrong answer, but a very funny answer. The group laughed loud and long.

(I'm sure that an immensely exaggerated version of this incident will be recounted at the next family get-together, so I'm bracing myself for the eventuality by plotting my revenge in advance.)

Mary Margaret Mahoney was my first true love. She was the proverbial "older woman." She was about my Uncle Dave's age, and in fact, I think they attended school together. Her age placed her out of the range of my charms because I moved into a new dimension of school life just as she was moving out.

For example, when I was in Mrs. Hawkins' room with the first, second, and third graders; she was in Mrs. Hoffman's room with the fourth, fifth, and sixth graders. When I went into the fourth grade, she went into Junior High, and when I went into Junior High, she was riding the train to Elkview High School. Naturally, by the time I got to high school, she had graduated.

I first noticed what an attractive and desirable woman Mary Margaret was about the time I was in the sixth grade. For some strange reason, I suddenly went from not thinking about girls at all, to all I thought about was girls. It was a strange and wonderful transformation and Mary Margaret, an exciting ninth grader, had all the right features to move me in ways I had never been moved before.

Now, don't think that my attraction to Mary Margaret was purely hormonal. I loved her with a love more pure than any love in the history of mankind. The only thing that kept our relationship from being absolutely perfect was the fact that she did not know that I so much as existed. So, she was not only my first love, but my "secret love" as well. And, as shy as I was, it was to remain a secret until this very moment.

Mary Margaret lived up the hollow past our house, so I often plotted ways to wait for her to come by so we would "accidentally" meet and walk the two "blocks" to school together. But, alas, I most often trudged off to school with my uncle Ron and my brother Larry.

I tried numerous ploys: forgetting something I needed so I would have to look for it while the others went to school without me; needing to make a last minute correction to my homework that delayed me; and other schemes that I'd lie awake half the night dreaming up. But, all to no avail.

At this point in the story, perhaps I should tell you a little more about the kind of woman Mary Margaret Mahoney was. Other than being ravishingly beautiful, of course, Mary Margaret was . . . well, she was "different." I'm not sure quite how to explain it without you getting the wrong impression about her, but, for some reason, Mary Margaret was always in some kind of trouble. There were a number of well-known and often recounted "incidents." And, while the sheer number of these incidents meant that she had some type of problem with about everyone in Quick, she was most often in trouble with those in some position of authority.

Mary Margaret was an orphan who had come to Quick when she was very young to live with her aunt. The aunt, who was quite young and flamboyant herself, took a very *liaise faire* attitude toward rearing Mary Margaret. She allowed Mary Margaret to do pretty much anything she wanted to do. Most of us kids in Quick took notice of this and greatly admired Mary Margaret for her good fortune.

But, I always felt that Mary Margaret never took advantage of her situation, mostly because her aunt was so lenient that she couldn't. When one of the Mary Margaret incidents occurred and she got caught doing something she shouldn't be doing, her aunt would simply say "Girls will be girls," and let it pass.

Now that I think about it, I feel that the Mary Margaret incidents were not so much some form of rebellion but were more the result of her curiosity. She just wanted to know about life. She wanted to experience it for herself and not live it vicariously like the rest of us. And I think her aunt's reaction to the incidents reflected the kind of love and trust that existed between the two of them. I always had the feeling that Mary Margaret would never do anything to hurt her aunt or to let her down. I envied the relationship, but I'm not sure I'd want that kind of responsibility as a child.

Based on some rather hard evidence, all the parents in Quick, and most of us kids, thought that Mary Margaret would end up in jail or worse. The "hard evidence" was the large number of notable incidents in which Mary Margaret was involved.

There was the "Fire in the Girl's Room" incident that led to a three-day suspension from Quick Junior High School after she got caught smoking in the girl's bathroom. (Actually, she would not have gotten caught had she not been careless about throwing the lighted cigarette in the trash. She threw it in there to avoid detection when she thought she heard one of the teachers approaching. By the time she found out that it was just another student, it was too late and the bathroom was full of smoke.)

Then there was the "Under the Bridge" incident, which, as we were told, was Mary Margaret's first step toward becoming an alcoholic. "Under the bridge" is where Mary Margaret had sneaked off to with two bottles of beer she had absconded from her aunt's refrigerator. She really didn't get drunk like everyone said. And she probably wouldn't have gotten caught that time either, if it hadn't been for the boy who had dared her to drink a bottle of beer. When she dared him back, he accepted. So she drank one bottle and he drank the other.

Unfortunately, he went home and threw up right in the middle of the living room. Then he told his parents that she had forced him to drink it and poor Mary Margaret was in trouble again.

There was also the "Trick-Or-Treat" incident which did major damage to the undercarriages of three automobiles, caused about a dozen "teen-age delinquents" to have to hide out in the woods over night, and brought a Kanawha County Deputy Sheriff to Quick to restore law and order and to ensure that the perpetrators were brought to justice. When the dust settled, it turned out (to no one's surprise) that Mary Margaret was the ring-leader of the group.

Now, I don't want you to think that everything related to Mary Margaret was totally negative. In her role as the person from Quick most likely to end up on the FBI's Ten Most Wanted List, she was often held up to the rest of us as a role model of how *not* to be.

But, in spite of dire predictions and to the total disappointment of many who believed in both civic and divine justice, Mary Margaret never actually served "time."

I guess it was predestined that I should be attracted to Mary Margaret. You see, like her, I was different too. Except that my difference is physical. I have red hair.

Those of you who do not have red hair will only snicker at this idea, but it's time you became sensitized to the issue. Redheads know the price of being different.

I hated being a redhead. I felt conspicuous and unattractive. No one says "Redheads have more fun." No one says "Tall, redheaded, and handsome." Instead, we hear things like "Better dead than red on the head" and "Redhead, wet-the-bed, five cents a cabbage head."

When you're growing up with red hair, it's bad enough putting up with these insults from the other kids. But adults are even worse. They don't even have to say anything. They just come up to you and rub you on the head.

And if they do say something, they will ask you one of life's stupidest questions: "Where'd you get that red hair?" I never knew what to say.

There was also some talk about a mysterious "milkman" who might be the source of my red hair. When I was little, I was always confused about that one. Especially since we didn't even have a milkman. But if we had, I didn't know how he could possibly have anything at all to do with my red hair.

The reason that having red hair is so traumatic is that when you're a kid, the one thing you want least in life is to be different, even in the smallest way, from all the rest of the kids in the world. And if you are different, you certainly don't want anyone calling attention to the difference.

Rugged individualism simply does not exist for children, any more than it does for teenagers or adults. All of life is a striving to be just like everyone else. You may want to have *more* than anyone else, but you don't want to be different.

I had two very close friends when I was growing up that I spent a lot of time with. One was my uncle Ron, who, although not tall, dark, and handsome, was nevertheless dark and handsome.

In grade school, Ron was Mrs. Hawkins' pet. He got to conduct the band, while I was relegated to the lowly role of playing the sticks. I remember all through school, the attention Ron gave his black wavy hair while my thick red mop just stood up in all directions.

While I never had any hope of awaking one day to find my hair had suddenly turned black, I did have hopes it might be more like my other close friend: my cousin Jerry. Jerry was tall, blond, and handsome, and I thought that, with the right amount of sun, my red hair might bleach to blond. My eyebrows grew blond in the sun; the hair on my forearms grew blond in the sun; but the hair on my head stayed red.

I thought about giving it a little help by applying hydrogen peroxide, but I was afraid to try it. I had heard that it might turn red hair bright orange. I felt conspicuous enough the way it was. Why make matters worse?

By the time I was in the sixth grade and madly in love with Mary Margaret, I was very aware of being different and I was aware that I was different in a way that I could not change. I was also aware of the cost in personal esteem and confidence that being different was having on my life.

So, maybe that was why I was attracted to Mary Margaret. Maybe it was because we both knew the cost of being different – a kind of shared inner torture between soul mates.

Then again, maybe it was just hormonal.

I learned one of life's hard lessons during the time I was so much in love with Mary Margaret. It was shortly after the "Stolen Mine Pony" incident (or was it the "Bad Word in Church" incident?). Several of the kids at school were talking about her and making fun of the things she did. I'm sure they were just repeating what they had heard their parents say – the same things my parents were saying to me – but it bothered me to hear them say things out loud and in public about the woman I loved.

As I stood there, I felt a great inner struggle. I caught myself wanting to be part of this group, to join in and make fun of her. After all, I needed their acceptance.

But, I also thought of Jesus and the "Woman Caught in Adultery" incident. He would not have stood idly by while this group "cast stones" at Mary Margaret. I knew what I should do. I should speak up for her. And I would, I knew I would, if only the opportunity presented itself.

Then one of the older boys said something crude about Mary Margaret, and everyone laughed. When he noticed I wasn't laughing, he turned and said "What's the matter, Red. Maybe she's a friend of yours." So I laughed, too.

Immediately, it was as if the rooster had crowed. I was aware of my betrayal and I burned with shame. I turned and walked away.

The incident bothered me for days. I kept thinking about it – about what I should have done and what I should have said. I relived it over and over. And as I did, it took on a greater dimension.

In my fantasy version, she is there – just out of sight of the group. I challenge the older boy and make the group (which includes a few parents and teachers by this time) see how wrong they are about Mary Margaret. My words are persuasive, but the older boy laughs at me and calls me "Red." I knock him out cold with one mighty blow. Then, as the crowd stares in admiration, she reveals herself. She comes to me, embraces me, and we walk away hand in hand together.

There were other versions of this fantasy, even one in which I get killed, but I liked this one the best.

On Saturday, about a week after the playground incident, I had to go out to my grandparent's farm to help them for the day. It was about a four-mile walk and I had plenty of time to think about how I had betrayed the woman I loved, and about myself. Self-loathing is not a pretty sight, nor an especially uplifting experience. But when you're a teenager, it can certainly be gratifying.

As I walked along, wallowing in self-pity, I suddenly began to see things differently. I began to realize that God loved and accepted me the way I was, and that I should do the same thing. So what if I was a red-haired, freckle-faced kid? So what if there were other guys better looking than I am, or better at baseball or other sports? I was me. I was a unique and valuable person and it was stupid to want to be anything other than who I was.

It was a great insight for someone my age and it changed my life. For one thing, it gave me the courage to make my own way in life, even if it was different from what others would have chosen for me. For another thing, it helped me get over Mary Margaret (but not right away).

Several years later, I think it was the summer after my senior year in high school, I saw Mary Margaret for the last time. She had come back to visit her aunt. She was walking around Quick, talking to people she had known, many of whom still remembered all the "incidents," but who by now were willing to allow for the changes that come with maturity.

I was working in the yard when she came by our house. She stood in the road and we talked a while, then she came up on the porch and we sat and talked some more. By now she had matured a lot and had become, it seemed to me, a very wise person. And she had some good advice for another teenager who, like herself, was trying to move beyond the confining atmosphere of a small hillbilly town and make something of himself in the world.

She told me about the things she felt that she had done right and clued me in on some of the things she felt she could have done better. She never mentioned any of the "incidents." They were insignificant in the light of a much greater world.

Mary Margaret had moved to Ohio where she was working her way through college. She had very little financial help, so, after three years of taking as many classes as she could while holding down a full-time job, she had completed the equivalent of three semesters. She was very proud of what she was doing and she was pleased to hear that I had enrolled in college and would be going to school in the fall.

At some point in the conversation Mary Margaret said something that I remembered but have never fully understood. I know I never took it to heart and lived by it the way she did.

I'm sure I can't quote it exactly, and I don't remember if she said that she had heard it, or read it, or had just made it up herself. What she said was to the effect that, "no one ever amounts to anything of significance by being just like everyone else."

To someone who is open to such a statement and who is prepared to live by it, I'm sure that it would be life changing. But I can tell you that although I remember what she said and thought of it often, her words had little or no real effect on my life. Even though I had come to terms with being different several years before, I still lived with a residue of hope that one day I'd wake up and I'd no longer have red hair.

Even now, I think that residue of hope still resides deep in my psychic, but now I know that it really will happen. One of these days I'll wake up and my hair will be grey!

Over the years, I have come to see how Mary Margaret exemplified the philosophy that no one amounts to anything of significance by being just like everyone else. She certainly made her mark in Quick by being different from the rest of us.

But I have also come to realize that she was not talking about childhood pranks and the dumb things we kids do when we're growing up. She was talking about a significant philosophy of life; a way of living each day so that one is not restricted by attempts to conform to the petty rules of society. Instead, it is a philosophy that actually encourages a person to explore new avenues of living in hope of finding something personally gratifying, no matter what the cost and no matter what others think or say about you.

When Aunt Kay said Mary Margaret's name that Saturday afternoon, I'm not sure what aspect of her life came flooding into my mind. Maybe in that moment, everything I knew about Mary Margaret flashed before my eyes, or maybe I remembered only those final moments we spent together on the porch as she tried so hard to send me forth into the world believing that if I were ever to amount to anything I'd have to stop trying to be just like everyone else.

Whatever it was, what happened when I heard her name caused me a lot of concern. As I sat there, with a group of people waiting for me to answer a question I didn't hear, I was wondering why, when I heard Mary Margaret's name, I saw the face of Jesus.

It deeply troubled me for the rest of that day, and for weeks to come. I tried to figure it out. Certainly Mary Margaret was not Jesus. I don't know that she was ever very religious. But, when her name was spoken, there in my mind, as clear as day, was the face of Jesus.

A few months later I was in a restaurant with my friend Brent. It was an all-night restaurant where we had gone to have a cup of coffee and a piece of pie, and plan the part of our church's worship service that he and I are responsible for. We were about the only people in the restaurant and neither of us was in a hurry. I had once again been thinking of Mary Margaret and the face of Jesus incident, so I told him about it.

"Why would I have seen the face of Jesus?" I asked.

He smiled. "Seems pretty simple to me."

"Really?"

"Sure," he said. "Who do you think most exemplifies Mary Margaret's philosophy?"

Receiving sudden insight is a wonderful experience. In a single moment of time, I saw what my subconscious mind had known for many years. Jesus is the true example of a person who made his mark in the world by not being just like everybody else.

"You see," Brent continued, "we have this image of Jesus that is very different from what was going on in Israel during his lifetime. We've always been told that Jesus is the person we should most be like. He's held up to us as a role model of all that is good and pure. But that simply was not the case in his hometown while he was alive."

"I see what you mean," I said. "There were probably mothers and fathers all over Nazareth who pointed Jesus out as an example of totally unacceptable behavior."

"And with what they felt were good reasons," Brent added. "But rather than do what other people felt was acceptable, he did what he felt was right, and that made him significantly different."

We were silent for a moment.

"But he wasn't *trying* to be significant," I said, interrupting the silence.

"No. He was only trying to help others find abundant life."

We finished our work, our coffee, and our pie, and headed for the parking lot.

"Whatever happened to Mary Margaret?" Brent asked. "Did she ever amount to anything significant?"

"I'm sure she would have," I told him. "If she had lived."

"She died?"

"Yeah. It's a sad story," I said. "After she graduated from college, she took a job working with the very poor people of southern West Virginia. Sometime in the early 1970's, I think it was, there was a very heavy rain storm in the area and an old slag pond burst. The water roared down the hollow and swept away everything. There were three kids trapped in an old house trailer. She managed to get two of them to safety. When she went back for the third, a twenty-foot wall of water came through and . . ."

I stopped.

"Man!" Brent said.

"They found her body about eight miles down stream. Tangled in the upper limbs of a tree."

"That is a very sad story," Brent acknowledged.

"Yeah," I said. "Every time I think about it, I think 'what a waste.'"

There was nothing more to say. Brent headed for his car and I headed for mine. I opened the door, got in, and started the motor. I sat there for a few moments, thinking about what Brent and I had talked about; that Jesus was significantly different, not because he was trying to be either significant or different, but because he was trying to help others find a better way to live.

And that's when it happened again. Only this time, as I thought about the life of Jesus, I saw the face of Mary Margaret Mahoney.

The Resurrection of Uncle Ron

1 The first day of the week cometh Mary Magdalene early, when it was yet dark, unto the sepulchre, and seeth the stone taken away from the sepulchre.

2 Then she runneth, and cometh to Simon Peter, and to the other disciple, whom Jesus loved, and saith unto them, They have taken away the Lord out of the sepulchre, and we know not where they have laid him.

3 Peter therefore went forth, and that other disciple, and came to the sepulchre.

4 So they ran both together: and the other disciple did outrun Peter, and came first to the sepulchre.

5 And he stooping down, and looking in, saw the linen clothes lying; yet went he not in.

6 Then cometh Simon Peter following him, and went into the sepulchre, and seeth the linen clothes lie,

7 And the napkin, that was about his head, not lying with the linen clothes, but wrapped together in a place by itself.

8 Then went in also that other disciple, which came first to the sepulchre, and he saw, and believed.

John 20:1 - 8
King James Version

THE DANES WERE such a lovely young couple – our new pastor and his wife. He was handsome. She was pretty. And they both were, in the words of Aunt Lorraine, "debonair." They were in their early twenties, just graduated from college. This was his first church.

Everyone in Quick simply loved our new pastor and his wife and we felt very lucky to have them – even though they only stayed a few months.

One of our new pastor's trademarks, besides his lovely wife, was his car. It was a sporty and brightly painted convertible – an American-made luxury car that was bought for him by his somewhat wealthy father. Even though it was five or six years old, it was better than most of the cars in Quick. The car made him popular, especially with the young people, and when he drove through Quick everyone knew who he was.

There was, however, one dissenter in our midst and that was Aunt Lorraine. Aunt Lorraine wasn't really our aunt. She was actually not related to us at all. She just arrived one day "out of the blue," or so it seemed to us, to live with my grandparents. I guess that's how she got the "aunt" in Aunt Lorraine.

After coming to Quick, Aunt Lorraine got saved at our church and became actively involved. She was probably in her early thirties, not at all attractive, a little over weight, and was what my Uncle Kester referred to as "not playing with a full deck."

However, there was one thing Aunt Lorraine could do superbly – faint. She could swoon in the most dramatic fashion imaginable. It was a wonderful trick which my sister Beverly tried to imitate every time Mom asked her to do some distasteful chore. Aunt Lorraine's timing was impeccable and it always attracted a lot of attention.

That is, until the new pastor arrived. After a couple of fainting spells in church, Brother Dane took her aside and told her that if she fainted one more time, she would not be allowed back in the church.

That was strike one. Strike two was the "devil-inspired conspiracy" between the pastor and the Sunday School Superintendent to give Aunt Lorraine's Grades 1 to 6 Girls Sunday School Class to Mrs. Jackson.

These could have been forgiven. But the clincher – the unpardonable sin – Strike Three! – came when one of the new young men who started coming to church after the Danes arrived was appointed President of the Young People's Society – a role that Aunt Lorraine had assumed shortly after her arrival, although she was never officially elected to the position.

When Brother Dane announced the appointment of the new Young People's Society President, Aunt Lorraine turned to my grandmother and, quoting one of her favorite TV characters, announced: "This means war!"

There was, for a church our size, quite an influx of young people who came because of the Danes. These were older young people, 18, 19, and 20, (I was 14 or 15 at the time) whose parents attended and who had been on the fringe of the church all of their lives but had never attended with any degree of regularity.

Now they were coming on a regular basis and being given positions of leadership. Even though they were "outsiders" to the church, the young people fit in quite well with the new pastor and his wife since these young people were, as Aunt Lorraine was quick to point out, "debonair" too.

Aunt Lorraine was the only one who found an unfavorable meaning in the term "debonair" when it was applied to the new pastor and to the young people he attracted. Most of us didn't know what the word meant or even how to spell it, but we knew that, as she used the term, it was not a respectable thing to be. I looked it up in the dictionary and saw that the list of synonyms included suave and sophisticated. I stopped right there. I didn't want to have to look up the meanings of a lot of other words I didn't know.

As the rift grew, Aunt Lorraine christened the Danes and their new group of young people "the Debonairs." Even if she was a few cards short, Aunt Lorraine could still come up with some good zingers now and then. She could be both witty ("Maybe I could get the Debonairs to sing backup for me some Sunday morning.") and biting ("The pastor, his pretty wife, and all of his young dumb Debonairs are going to bust hell wide open.").

The Young Debonairs, as they came to be affectionately known – to themselves and to everyone in the church – were fully accepted and their presence was applauded as a symbol of future growth for the church. These, we were told, are the leaders of tomorrow.

The Young Debonairs themselves thought all of this was very amusing and gladly accepted their new name. The parents of the Debonairs, many of whom attended the church and who had been requesting prayer for their sons and daughters for years, were thrilled.

Aunt Lorraine, on the other hand, was not thrilled. She saw the ready acceptance of these "reprobates who aren't even saved" as a weakening of the moral fiber of the church. Her opposition to the group and her stinging criticisms were ignored and often laughed at even by those of us, who, like her, were being pushed aside to give the spotlight to this new group. Even though we wouldn't admit it, in our hearts we knew she was right – that they were only temporary and would be part of the "great falling away" in the last days (or as soon as the Danes left, whichever came first).

While Aunt Lorraine was suffering outrageous misfortune at the hands of her enemies, others were of a different opinion – me for example. My greatest desire was to be accepted into this group and to become a Young Debonair myself.

Unlike "Aunt" Lorraine, Uncle Ron really is my uncle. He's two months older than I am and we grew up together. We were born in the same house, went to the same schools, lived in the same neighborhood (in fact, next door to each other), played on the same high school football team, and were the best of friends. Everyone knew that if you saw one of us, the other would be nearby. We did everything together.

And so it was on Good Friday that Ron and I, pretty much the only non-debonair teens in the church, joined the pastor and his wife, and the Young Debonairs to assemble the props for the most elaborate Easter Sunrise Celebration ever to occur in Quick, West Virginia, and probably within all of Kanawha County up to that time.

I was thrilled of course, seeing this as my opportunity to prove myself and become an inductee into this most favored group. Ron, on the other hand, was under the influence of Aunt Lorraine and did not bestow upon the undertaking the reverence it deserved. It was a holiday from school and the last thing he wanted was to be involved in a project where he had to work. As a result, Ron kept pestering me all day to leave and do something with him. Naturally I refused.

The father of one of the Debonairs had agreed to help, and the plan was to build a tomb with a stone covering the entrance. On cue, this stone would, without the apparent assistance of others, roll away to reveal an empty chamber – just like it did on Resurrection Morning.

The Young Debonairs would then enact two short dramas. The first would feature Mary Magdalene arriving at the tomb and encountering the angel who would tell her that Jesus had risen. The Debonairs got a big kick out of referring to Mary Magdalene as "Jesus' girlfriend," and laughed uproariously whenever it was said. The girl who was to be Mary Magdalene said a couple of crude things which drew even more laughter. I laughed too. In fact I laughed at all of their jokes even though most of the time I didn't know what was so funny.

The second drama would feature two male Debonairs as Peter and John who rush to the tomb to find only the strips of cloth that had bound the body and the linen that covered his face.

The tomb that would serve as the backdrop for the dramas was the sealed entrance to an old coal mine. It was a hundred yards up a very steep hill above the home of the Debonair family whose father was constructing the "Stone." By law and for safety's sake, a huge concrete slab completely sealed the entrance to the mine, but there was a small overhang that left a space in front of the slab that could be used for the tomb.

The "Stone" was, of course, not stone. We had lots of rocks in the area, but a stone large enough to cover the entrance would have been so heavy that we would have had to use dynamite to move it away from the entrance (an idea that Uncle Ron espoused with a certain amount of glee).

Instead, the Stone was made of plywood and two-by-fours. The Debonair dad had spent several late nights in his workshop creating this masterpiece. The plywood was cut in a circle and the two-by-fours were used for the frame. To make the Stone stable, plywood was nailed to both the front and back of the frame. When finished and painted, the Stone looked somewhat like a giant misshapen millstone without its center hole.

And it only weighed slightly less than a rock of equal size.

It took all of us an hour to lug and drag the thing up the hill and put it over the opening. Of course it didn't fit, so we spent the next hour digging around the entrance to make the opening fit the Stone. At one point the Stone looked like it might topple forward but everyone rushed to grab it and hold it in place.

When all of the digging was done, the Stone fit snugly against the mouth of the mine. We stopped for lunch.

During lunch I tried to sit near a couple of Debonairs but Ron plopped down next to me. I had noticed that he hadn't done much work on the project. I had kept busy the whole time and I was sure the Debonairs were aware of my faithful service.

While we ate, a couple of the Debonairs talked with Ron and seemed to ignore me. As I watched them, I realized they liked him better than me. Most of the female Debonairs thought Ron was cute. Even though he was a lot younger than they were, I was sure that they'd let him join the group if he wanted to. But he didn't seem to care. He said they were just a bunch of phonies, but I'm sure that was just Aunt Lorraine talking. After all, she lived with his family. I was somewhat free of her influence and had a much more realistic perspective.

When lunch was over, Ron tried once again to lure me away from the project. But, like a good soldier, I continued to do what I felt was right. I just wished that the Debonairs would talk with me like they talked with Ron. After all, I was their true friend. Not him.

After lunch we began to develop the track in which the stone would move. The original plan was to rig chains and pulleys to move the Stone in an orderly and controlled fashion. A guy-wire would run to a nearby tree to ensure that the Stone stayed in its track.

But now it was nearly three o'clock in the afternoon, much too late in the day for a bunch as tired as we were to rig up the contraption, so it was decided to dig a trench and allow the Stone to roll a couple of feet down a slight incline and stop in the low spot. A large block of wood cut in the shape of a triangle would hold the Stone in place. The wooden block was fastened to a wire which ran through a buried pipe and away from the tomb. From a secret location, the Debonair Dad would pull the wire which would then pull the block out of the way and the stone would roll away from the entrance on its own momentum. It seemed like a good plan.

Of course it didn't work the first time we tried it, nor did it work the second. When it did work on about the eighth try we were sorry it did. Now we had to lift and push the massive monster back out of the low spot and into its place over the entrance.

After one more try we decided that it would work perfectly on the morning of the Easter Sunrise Celebration and Dramatic Presentation, or it wouldn't work at all. By this time we didn't really care. We were exhausted.

As we were pushing the Stone back over the entrance to the tomb, the female Debonairs rushed forward to halt the operation. It seems that the inside of the tomb needed work. They had to put a bench inside to show where the body had been placed. And they were still busy tearing sheets into strips to represent the cloth which had been wrapped around Jesus' body and which Peter and John would find in the tomb.

But rather than let the Stone slip back into its "open" position, we blocked it with rocks so we would only have to push it a short distance to get it into place. It now rested slightly open, but with enough room for the girls to get in and out.

As I began to clean and straighten the trench and cover the pipe that contained the wire, Ron came to try to get me to play one more time.

"Let's go," he whispered, "it's going to get dark." When I refused, he kicked dirt into Stone's trench.

"Knock it off, you little creep!" I said, more tired than angry. It was a line we'd heard in a movie and liked to use it on one another. As I said it, I heard a snicker and looked up to see that all of the Debonairs were watching us – and smiling.

Our English teacher had just finished a unit on Shakespeare and we had memorized a stanza that said that there is a tide in the affairs of men that, when taken at its utmost leads on to great reward (or something like that). I suddenly realized that my tide had come.

I turned back to Ron and thrust the shovel handle toward his face. "Why don't you grow up?" I told him trying to sound angry. He seemed surprised at my over-reaction. But instead of responding, he turned the other cheek and simply walked away.

I subtly glanced back at the Debonairs who were laughing among themselves, then turned my attention to the trench as I continued my work and tried to hide the smile that was spreading across my face. I had shown my true loyalties and I knew I would be rewarded. After a few moments I looked up again. One of the Debonairs was watching me. He gave me a wink and I winked back. I knew I was making progress and would likely be accepted into the group as the youngest of the Debonairs.

We worked quickly, but in another hour it was dark. The Debonairs had intended to practice their dramas, but it was too late. Besides, tomorrow was Saturday and they'd have plenty of time to practice. And we could even do a little more work on getting the Stone to roll away on cue. We gathered the tools and took one last look around. We were proud of our efforts.

As we started down the hill, someone remembered the Stone had not been rolled into place. Several of us went back and closed the tomb. Then we were finished.

There was a party for the young people that night. I was allowed to stay. I only embarrassed myself really, really badly one time. Then, when Sister Dane made fun of me for blushing, I took her comments as a joke – even though they didn't seem so at the time.

Later that evening as I was getting ready for bed, I thought about how I had proven myself in front of the Debonairs and although I didn't feel fully accepted, I knew that my time would come. The very embarrassing moment was playing itself out again in my mind when the phone rang.

I answered. It was my grandmother wanting to know if Ron was there. When I said no, she asked me when I had last seen him. Suddenly his face flashed before my eyes, staring at me past the handle of the shovel, then turning and walking away.

"At the tomb," I said quickly.

"Do you know where he went?"

"No," I said.

She was quiet for a moment. "Okay," she said and hung up the phone.

At about midnight, a Kanawha County Sheriff's patrol car pulled up in front of my grandparent's house and two young Deputies got out. They were greeted by a small group who had gathered in the front yard to wait for their arrival. I stood in the back of the crowd.

My grandfather, grandmother, and Aunt Lorraine came out of the house and joined the others who parted to allow them to come through to talk to the Deputies. My grandfather became the spokesperson, answering questions about Ron's disappearance.

I only remember one of those questions: Would he have had a reason to run away? My grandfather said he didn't think so. As he answered, the Debonairs who had winked at me earlier turned and looked at me. The look pierced me to my heart and suddenly I knew how Peter felt when he got caught denying the Lord.

After my grandfather said he didn't think Ron had a reason to run away, the Deputy was quiet for a moment, then shook his head, a serious look coming across his face.

"It's probably nothing to worry about," he said, then added "but you might want to prepare yourself for the worst."

At this point Aunt Lorraine performed her most magnificent swoon ever. With the grace and agility of a ballerina she seemed to lift herself a foot or more off the ground and, almost in slow motion, came down in the arms of the better looking of the two Deputies. Had it not been such a serious occasion, we might have given her a standing ovation. Well, at least an ovation since we were already standing.

The next day was a time of trial and tribulation. Some people answered the phone or made calls while others organized search parties. A prayer vigil was organized at all three churches in Quick. Concerned friends and loved ones brought food for the family and the curious came just to get a look at the suffering. Naturally the Easter Sunrise Extravaganza drama practice was canceled.

Rumors abounded. Ron was seen hitchhiking north on U. S. 119, south on the West Virginia Turnpike, and both east and west on Route Sixty. There was a rumor that he had been kidnapped and was being held for $50,000 ransom.

While others searched for Ron in obvious places, I looked in the secret places that only he and I knew - deep in the woods where we played together, enjoying the many carefree hours of our youth. I found a quiet spot in a pine forest which had often served as our fort and lay on the soft needles, staring up through the lofty limbs of the pines and reflecting on life with Uncle Ron.

I knew the rumors about Ron were not true. I knew Ron well enough to know that if he had run away he would have taken his dad's car. He didn't care that much for walking and he would never have hitchhiked alone. It always embarrassed him to thumb a ride so he'd let me be the one to stick out the thumb.

No, there was really only one answer. Uncle Ron was dead. In my mind I saw him in a ditch somewhere. I don't know why, but a ditch just seemed the most appropriate place - a small ditch beside a road, maybe up toward Sanderson.

The thought of him dead in the ditch tore my heart apart because I knew that I was the one who had put him there - I, the friend he trusted; the friend he wanted to spend his last day with, playing games instead of building a tomb for some dumb Easter play for a bunch of phonies who wouldn't stick it out with us in a crisis. They just laughed at us – and not behind our backs either – to our faces. But Ron knew. He knew what they were like. And I betrayed him, like Judas, and denied him, like Peter.

As I thought of Uncle Ron and the good times, now gone forever, tears became sobs, not so much for him, for he was with God, but for me – the betrayer. I now had a profound understanding of poor Judas, hurling the pieces of silver back across the floor, then clutching a rope and looking for just the right tree.

The more I thought about it, the more it tore at me, ripping away the very fiber of my soul, causing me to suffer the anguish and grief that comes with mourning the loss of innocence. It was just the thing to catapult a forlorn teenager into absolute and utter self-pity. In other words, it felt great!

Late in the day on Saturday the decision was made to go ahead with the Easter Sunrise Extravaganza. It would be somewhat subdued of course, but after some debate it was felt that the work of the Young Debonairs should not be wasted. Easter, after all, was Easter – a time to celebrate, a time to think of the future when the dead would rise and we'd all join together in the clouds. Unspoken, but implied, was the feeling that the Great Resurrection Morning would likely be the next time we'd see Uncle Ron.

And so, as the late April sky showed the early signs of dawn, a larger than might have otherwise been expected group of weary pilgrims assembled and climbed the hill to the tomb that, from times past, they knew would be empty. We stood in silence, heavy hearted and staring at the ground, as the ceremony began. We didn't need a program to know how it would play out: the Stone would roll away, the two dramas would be presented, we'd sing a couple of Easter songs, and then we'd go home.

At the appointed time, the signal was given and the Debonair Dad pulled the wire to release the block. The Stone did not move. There was some whispering among the Debonairs about sending someone to give the Stone a nudge, but just then a muffled sound was heard and the Stone slowly turned, moving about half of its intended distance before it stopped.

This was the signal for the first line of the first drama and the actor Debonair called out: "Behold the empty . . . ." He stopped. When he did, we raised our eyes from the ground and looked at him. He was staring toward the tomb, so we turned our attention there, toward which he was pointing.

To our amazement we discovered that the tomb was indeed not empty. There, before our very eyes and still wrapped in strips of cloth in an attempt to keep warm, stood a very sheepish looking Uncle Ron.

A great cry went up from the group as everyone rushed to the tomb. Everyone except, naturally, Aunt Loraine, who fainted; this time for real.

It was a moment of great excitement with hugs and kisses and tears. Someone in the crowd began to sing an Easter song and everyone joined in. We sang with new enthusiasm because that which we had only heard about in the past, we now had witnessed in our own lives. And so, for a half hour or more, we rejoiced in the resurrection of Uncle Ron.

After the celebration, we encircled Uncle Ron, seemingly trying to get as close as possible, and began to go down the hill. We were halfway down the steep incline when someone noticed there was a slight movement of the Stone. We turned to look just in time to see it suddenly come free of whatever had kept it from opening fully. It rolled a short distance along the trench and settled with a thud into the bottom of the low spot. We stood in frozen amazement at the sight, then breathed a sigh of relief.

Several people turned and again started down the hill until someone in the back said "uh-oh." When we turned back, we saw the stone had begun to slowly twist. As we watched, it turned until it was now aimed down the hill. We scattered, running to the left and the right to clear a path for the Stone, which had now taken on a life of its own. Then we waited to see if it would do what it looked like it might do. We stood, all eyes fixed on the Stone, which just sat there rather precariously, trying to make up its mind whether to roll or to topple.

It decided to roll.

It rolled slowly for the first few feet, then it suddenly gained momentum and shot down the hill at great speed. At first, it was aimed directly at the house, but it hit a stump which turned it so that it was now headed toward the work shed. Then it hit a rock which turned it away from the shed and sent it on a path that would take it through the side yard between the house and the shed.

As it crushed through the backyard fence and headed across the side yard, there was a sigh of relief. It would miss both the house and the shed. That's when it suddenly dawned on us that the preacher's sporty and brightly painted American-made luxury convertible bought for him by his somewhat wealthy father lay directly in its path.

We stood helpless, our hands over our mouths as the Stone lunged through the yard toward the front fence, the road, and the doomed car. I glanced at the preacher. He was as white as the strips of cloth that had been used to wrap the body of Jesus.

The front fence turned out to be an immovable object for the Stone's irresistible force and with the angle of incidence being equal to the angle of reflection; the stone veered slightly to the right and missed the car by a good two inches.

The pastor fainted.

It was a good faint and almost as dramatic as when Aunt Lorraine had fainted into the arms of the good looking Sheriff's Deputy the night Uncle Ron, in one of his joking moods, had sneaked unseen into the empty tomb.

Redwing Is My Brother

13 Then were there brought unto him little children, that he should put his hands on them, and pray: and the disciples rebuked them.

14 But Jesus said, Suffer little children, and forbid them not, to come unto me: for of such is the kingdom of heaven.

15 And he laid his hands on them, and departed thence.

Matthew 19: 13 - 15
King James Version

"IT'S THE SHERIFF of Kanawha County," said Judy over the intercom.

"The who?"

"He said to tell you: 'it's the Sheriff of Kanawha County.'"

"The Sheriff of Kanawha County?" I mumbled to myself. Then I remembered who the Sheriff of Kanawha County was.

"The Sheriff of Kanawha County!" I said with excitement. "Thanks, Judy."

I punched the blinking button.

"Howdy, Sher'f," I said, trying to recall my best West Virginia accent.

"Howdy there Mr. Smith-goes-to-Warshington."

"Howzit goin', Sher'f."

"Great! Couldn't be better."

I dropped the accent. "Mom said you'd been elected sheriff. Congratulations."

"See! There you go. You don't even sound like a West Virginian no more."

"I know. I took speech lessons. Norma Berkley taught me not to say 'Mah boosh's on far.' Now I say 'm-eye bush is on fire!'"

"They ruint ye!"

"Yeah. Just another good ole West Virginia boy gone bad. Anyway, I thought you retired from the law enforcement business. That's what you said at the last reunion."

"Well, I did. Twenty years and one day with the State Police."

"Twenty years and a day?"

"That's right. It's not that I was anxious to get out. I just had other plans."

"Like?"

"Being Sheriff of our home county. I started here, y'know. I was a 'depity' for two years before I went with the state. It's like coming back home."

"Well, congratulations. I'm sure you're doing a good job."

"Tryin' to. But, enough about me. I called to find out if you're coming home this summer for our high school reunion. It's a big one, y'know."

"Yep. In fact, I'm planning to be there a few days early. I want to do some visiting with the folks. Haven't been home for a couple of years."

"Yeah. That's what your mom said. I called her to get your phone number. Anyhow, I'd like you to stop by my office. I got somethin' that belongs to you and I'd like to return it."

"Belongs to me?"

"Yeah."

There was a moment of silence.

"Well, what is it?"

"You'll see when you get here. I think you'll find it very interesting."

"Can you give me a hint?"

"Nope. I'd like for it to be a su'prise."

I paused. "Well, okay. I'll give you a call when I get in town and set an appointment."

"No need. Just drop by. I'm always here."

Bob Reilly, the Sheriff of Kanawha County, was a friend and fellow high school football player. He was very analytical and methodical, but I never thought of him as a law enforcement officer. I don't know why, but he just didn't seem to have the type of personality I imagined that police officers have. He was very mild-mannered, and when it comes to leadership, he was a guard not a quarterback. But, he was very successful as an investigator for the State Police and was evidently an excellent leader in his role as Sheriff.

At our twentieth high school reunion Bob told several of us a story that really impressed me and it's one I've told to my friends many times. He said he had been a highway patrolman for several years and had gotten to the place that he wanted something more challenging. He applied for a job as an investigator and got the promotion. But some of his superiors didn't think he had what it took to be a good investigator.

A short time later, the home of a wealthy Charleston family was burglarized. The owner of the house awoke and confronted the burglar. There was a struggle, the homeowner was killed, and the robber fled. Bob was assigned the case. It was his first big case, and if he could crack it, he'd silence his critics.

Within a couple of days, he had arrested a suspect, but everyone felt the evidence was weak. Most of the evidence was very circumstantial, including a high school ring found at the scene of the crime. The ring was from the suspect's high school, and his initials were engraved inside the ring. As he interrogated the suspect, Bob said he casually handed him the ring and asked if he'd ever seen it.

"When he looked up at me," Bob said to me and the other members of his rapt audience, "I could see the whole story in his eyes. And he knew I could. He told us everything right there."

Bob paused for a moment to let his words sink in, then punched his point home. "The eyes really are the windows to the soul," he said. "They tell you everything you want to know."

As I hung up the phone, what I really wanted to know was what the heck Bob had that belonged to me. I hadn't the foggiest idea. I shrugged and tried to forget it, but it bugged me off and on for the next several weeks. In fact, I was so curious about it that the day after I arrived in Quick to visit my folks, I made the trek to his office in Charleston to find out what it was.

I parked in a visitor's space in back of the court house and followed the sign down the stairs into the basement to the Sheriff's office.

I opened the door and walked in. I was greeted by a bright-eyed young deputy who was impeccably dressed in a dark blue uniform.

"May I help you?" she asked in a deep central West Virginia brogue that brought back a flood of memories.

"I'm here to see the sheriff."

"Do you have an appointment?"

"He said t' jus' drop by."

I felt the language coming back. Me and my West Virginia accent had been the butt of a lot of jokes over the years. I'd worked hard to change the way I talked, but it was amazing how quickly the accent returned when I came back for a visit.

"Your name?" she asked.

"Richard Smith."

"Just a moment, Mr. Smith."

She disappeared through an office door. Almost immediately, Bob emerged, a big smile spreading across this face.

"My-My," he said. "The wanderin' boy's come home t' the hills." He shook my hand warmly.

Bob looked great. He was trim and muscular, and very dashing in his uniform. It's guys like him that make a desk jockey like me *not* want to show up at a high school reunion.

"This is my old pal and fellow football teammate," he told the deputy.

He looked me over. "You could'a used some of that weight back then," he said with a wink. "Why, you'd probably have been all-state."

We laughed. He took me by the arm. "You look great!" he said, leading me toward the office door.

"Hold everything," he told the deputy. "We got some catching up to do."

I felt like an honored guest.

He closed the door and gestured to a chair. It was not a big office and the furniture was mostly old and wooden. He had decorated pretty well. A large number of books on the

West Virginia State Code filled a floor to ceiling bookcase. One wall was covered with photos and awards.

"So, you still makin' movies?" he asked as he leaned against his desk.

"Well, it's all done with video now – 'video-based training' is what we call it"

"Yeah. We're using a lot of video ourselves. We even have some of them little cameras mounted in our cars."

He paused for a moment. I wanted to cut the small talk and find out what he had that belonged to me. But, then again, I didn't want too seem anxious.

"Yeah. It's amazing how it's changed the road-side manners of some of my officers, knowin' that they're on TV."

We laughed.

"How's your folks?"

"They're fine. Dad complains about all the grass he has to mow, and swears he's going to raise a smaller garden, but gardening and mowing the grass gives him something to do. He hates to be cooped up in the winter."

We talked on and on. Small talk. And all the while, I grew more anxious, wondering what he had that belonged to me and when he would get around to giving it back. There was a lull in the conversation.

"You said you had something that belonged to me," I said.

"Oh! Right! I nearly forgot."

He went around his desk, sat in his chair, opened a desk drawer, and pulled out an old weather beaten child-size cowboy hat. He put it on the desk in front of me.

"There it is."

I looked at the hat. Then I looked at Bob. He smiled at me from across the desk.

"A kid's cowboy hat?" I said, puzzled.

"Yep."

I looked back at the hat. This must be a mistake, I thought. I had never seen that hat before in my life. I was about to tell Bob that he was mistaken about the hat belonging to me, but I suddenly felt that the hat did seem vaguely familiar. It was as if a memory of that hat was somewhere in the back of my mind and that it was rushing toward the front of my mind at lightning speed.

When it got there, I remembered the hat. It really was my hat. I remember who gave it to me. And I remembered the last time I saw it.

I sat and stared at the hat, but my mind was many miles and many years away. I was thinking about a case of murder, about the statutes of limitations for murder and for being an accessory to murder, and the penalty for harboring a known criminal. I was wondering if I should insist on having a lawyer present, and if so, who would I call.

As I thought about these things, I also remembered the story of Bob's first big case. I wondered how many times over the years he had successfully used that same technique to beguile a criminal into confessing.

At the time Bob told the story, I was impressed by his cleverness. But now, as I sat staring at a piece of evidence that linked me to a murderer, I didn't dare look up. I knew that, across the desk, my old friend and fellow high school football teammate sat waiting for a peek into my troubled soul.

The last time I saw the hat was on a cold, cloudy late March afternoon in one of those years when Easter came early. I was spending my Easter vacation from high school helping my grandparents on their farm.

I jabbed the pitchfork into the hay and lifted a fork full, maneuvering it through a small opening and into the mangers for the cows.

As I spread it evenly between the two mangers, I looked up to see Grampa coming toward me. He was limping badly. I thought that the frown on his face was from the pain in his legs, but it wasn't.

"Old Barnie's got out," he called to me as he neared the barn. "Looks like he pushed over one of those old rotten fence posts and took off."

There were a lot of old rotten fence posts on the farm these days. It was simply impossible to keep up with the maintenance. Grampa bought the farm in the late 1920's with the workman's compensation settlement he got after his legs were badly burned in an accident at a smelting factory.

My dad was six years old when they moved here to the top of this mountain. He's told me many times how they rode the train to Trestle Crossing and then walked three miles up to the top of the mountain and the farm. My Grandma, a city girl who was born and raised in Charleston, complained the whole way. She thought buying the farm was a big mistake and didn't want to stay. Now, she wouldn't leave the place.

Grampa was an energetic young man when molten lead was accidentally spilled on both of his legs below the knees. He survived the burns, but he said that it was something about the lead that kept the wounds from healing. More than thirty years had passed since the accident, and his legs were still covered with large open sores. He had been to a number of noteworthy hospitals, including Johns Hopkins Hospital in Baltimore, but nothing could be done for him.

Every night he bandaged his legs, putting salve on the sores. They'd improve for a while, then they'd get worse. Right now they were very bad and that's why I was spending my Easter vacation helping out on the farm.

I generally worked here all summer, me and my cousin Jerry. The farm never made a very good living for the family. It was too hilly to plow and plant with a tractor, and, in places, it was even too steep for a team of horses.

Although I spent a lot of time here in the summer, l seldom came here to work during the winter. But they needed me to help out right now, to give Grampa a chance to get off his legs.

"You'd better go find him," Grampa said.

I pushed the pitchfork tines into the soft earth inside the barn and placed the handle against the wall. We walked out of the barn and looked down into the steep pasture where the horses grazed. Grampa pointed out the broken fence.

"Right over there," he said. "It's hard to tell how long he's been gone."

"I put him out this morning about eight," I said.

He pulled out his faithful pocket watch. "You'd better get started," he said, holding the watch out for me to see. "It's almost two o'clock now."

I looked at the watch. Ten till two. It seemed much later because of the overcast sky.

"They're predicting snow; say it might be heavy."

We walked back to the house so I could get my heavy coat. Grandma gave me a cup of hot coffee to warm me up. I slipped on the coat and gloves.

"Where's your cap?" asked Grampa.

"I forgot to bring it."

"Well you need something." He looked around the room. "Here take this."

He handed me the cowboy hat.

"It's way too small," I protested, handing it back to him.

He refused to take it.

"You'll need something. Better wear it."

I put it on. Even though it had been too big when Grampa first bought it for me, it was definitely too small now.

Grampa smiled. "Looks fine to me."

"Yeah!" I said, starting to take it off.

"You better take it. If it snows, it'll be a lot better than nothing."

We went out the door. Grampa stopped as I walked on toward the back gate.

"You ought to be able to pick up his tracks," Grampa said. I stopped and turned as I listened. "If he went up the hill, his shoes'll cut into the dirt pretty deep. If you don't see tracks, go around the side of the hill. If I know Barnie, he'll take the path of least resistance."

I nodded.

"If it starts to snow heavy, come on back. We'll find him tomorrow."

Once again I started for the gate.

"And if he's headed for Disappearance Ridge . . . ." Grampa let his voice trail off. I stopped and turned toward Grampa. We stared at each other for a moment. Even though we didn't say it, we were both thinking the same thing. We were both hoping Ole Barnie wasn't headed for Disappearance Ridge.

"Use your own judgment. But don't go too far, and mark your trail. You know how easy it is to . . . ."

He didn't finish the statement, but I knew what he meant. '. . . how easy it is to get lost out there.'

I nodded.

"Don't worry about that!" I said.

He smiled.

"Rest those legs," I told him. "I'll be back in time to get the cows in for milking."

"If you're not, Tish can handle it."

As I walked along the road to the horse pasture, I thought about the area that had been nicknamed "Disappearance Ridge." I'd been around this farm all my life, but the one place I'd never gone was Disappearance Ridge. And I had no desire to go there. Grampa claims he's been there once, back in the '30s, before he'd heard the stories; and it might be true. My dad says he and his brothers never went there, but they always talked about it a lot.

In fact, there are a lot of stories about that area. Disappearance Ridge is an extremely rugged mountainous area about two miles around the hill from my grandparent's farm. The area is supposedly haunted by the ghosts of a family of settlers who built an old log house out there and was clearing the land to farm. One cold winter night back in the 1800s the house burned, killing everyone in the family but the dog. Supposedly, on nights when there's a full moon, you can hear that old dog's mournful howl.

Over the years, there were also stories of hunters who wandered out onto Disappearance Ridge, following the barking of their coon hounds who had treed something out there.

Supposedly they never returned. The theory was that it wasn't the hunters' dogs that they had heard since their dogs showed up back home. It was the ghost dog that had drawn them to their destiny.

By the time I was growing up, people didn't say much about the area known as Disappearance Ridge. But I do remember one occasion when my dad and his brother talked about it. I was about twelve and we had come to the farm one cool fall morning for "Butchering Day." It was a yearly tradition that several of us would come out the Friday after Thanksgiving and butcher Grampa's big hog. It was my grandparent's meat for the winter.

My job was to gather the wood to make the fire, but I always wanted to be the one to shoot the hog. I don't know why. After spending the summer carrying heavy buckets of slop the one hundred yards from the house to the pig pin, why would I want to shoot him? I don't know, but I did.

Shooting was "Lit'lee's" job. "Lit'lee" was the family nickname for dad's next younger brother, Wilbur, who was six foot four and was called Lit'lee for the same reason that heavy men are sometimes called "Tiny." He did the shooting, which really only stunned the animal. Then Grampa "stuck" him with a large knife. That was an expert's job. It had to be done right or the hog would suffer.

On this day, as I worked, scraping the pig's skin – what I called "shaving the pig" – dad and his brother somehow got onto the subject of Disappearance Ridge.

"Johnny said he went there," said Lit'lee

"Nah. He's lying," said my dad.

"I really didn't believe him, but he swore it was true."

"He's too big a coward."

As I listened, I recalled other stories I'd heard about Disappearance Ridge. I knew I wasn't too big a coward to go there. But, I was glad we weren't going there that day.

"Why do they call it 'Disappearance Ridge'?" I asked.

"Because people disappear there," said Lit'lee. "And, it's supposed to be haunted by ghosts who like to eat children."

I stood and turned to look across the valley toward Disappearance Ridge.

"Don't tell him that," my dad said to Lit'lee. "People are *supposed* to have disappeared there," Dad reassured me. "But it's just a lot of superstitious nonsense."

Grampa took a break from butchering and wiped his forehead on his sleeve.

"No, it's true," he said. "Happened more than once. In the mid-30s, a 'coon hunter went in there after his dogs who had treed something. His buddies refused to go, but he laughed at them and went." Grampa paused and carefully looked at us. "He never came out," he said.

"I remember that," Dad said. "I went to school with his son."

"What about them deer hunters," said Lit'lee. "That was right after I came back from the war. Must have been '46 or '47."

"Someone said the sheriff's men didn't even want to go in there looking for them," said Dad. "They finally did, but they never found a trace of them. Not a trace!"

"I only talked to one man who I believed when he said he'd been to Disappearance Ridge," Grampa said. "Old Man Davidson. He was a fearless sort of a feller. He said it was really rugged in there. The hills are very rocky and almost like cliffs. Said it was ghostly quiet. He said there didn't seem to be a living creature of any kind in there. He claimed that he was looking for the chim'ley of that old house that burned down and killed those people, but it was so creepy and it spooked him so bad he gave up and came back out of there."

We all stood in silence looking toward Disappearance Ridge. There seemed to be a chill in the air. Finally, almost in a whisper, my dad said: "Not a trace." Then we went back to work.

Now, as I lowered the top two bars and stepped over the bottom bar, Dad's words came back to me. I shook them off.

We didn't have gates to the pastures; we used "bars." There were three bars that slipped into slots in the fence posts and could be removed and replaced. I put the top two bars back in place. If Barnie happened to come back before I did, I didn't want him to find the bars down.

I carefully made my way down the steep hill, crossed a small creek, and then went back up the hill a little way until I came to the broken fence post. I stepped across the wire, then tried to figure out which direction Barnie might have taken. Grampa was right. He took the path of least resistance. He also took the path most likely to lead to Disappearance Ridge.

The trail was very visible at first. His shoes made distinct impressions in the soft dirt. As I followed the path, I got the feeling that Barnie had somewhere to go in mind and was making a straight path to get there. Of course, being a horse, he'd never heard the stories about Disappearance Ridge.

I entered a wooded area. The trees were tall and sparse. After a short distance, the trail turned up the mountain and came out into one of the flatter areas along the side of the hill.

This field was one of the places we hayed in the summer. It was "relatively" level, but unfortunately the only way out of this field toward the barn was down a short, but very steep incline. And with a loaded sled, that presented a problem. Even though we used chains under the runners to braked the sled and held back on the load with our pitchforks, we always worried about running upon the horses.

One year, the sled ran onto the single tree of Grandpa's favorite little mare. She was down on her hind legs, and was snorting with fright.

It took a while, but we got the sled raised and freed the horse. After that, I always worried when we had to move a load of hay out of that field.

I surveyed the field to see which direction Barnie had taken. He had obviously moseyed his way through a corner of the field, taking time for some nourishment. Then he went out the upper end of the field and up the slope toward the top of the hill. Once again he seemed to be determined to get to a destination known only to him.

I followed his trail for another mile. Since I had entered an unfamiliar area, I carefully checked the surrounding terrain to make sure I could find my way back. The trail would be distinct for a while, and then almost disappear. I trudged on. It grew darker and darker as heavy snow clouds formed overhead. Finally I stopped. I knew instinctively that I had arrived at the entrance to Disappearance Ridge.

I thought about going back. It would be easy to follow Barnie's tracks back to the farm. We'd find him tomorrow. But I decided to keep going – for a little while at least.

The forest grew very dense. I wondered where a horse could possibly be going through this sort of terrain. I thought about the lost hunters, I thought about the snow, and I thought about the ghosts of dead children.

Suddenly I realized I had been walking and thinking but had not been watching for Barnie's tracks. I carefully searched the ground.

There were no tracks. I went back a short distance, studying the ground. No tracks. Next, I went a hundred yards to the left, but there was no sign of Barnie. I came back to the ridge, then went a hundred yards to the right. Nothing!

And it was starting to snow.

I carefully searched the horizon for a sign of something familiar. With all the back-tracking and the moves to the left and right, I had become disoriented. As I studied the terrain, I began to realize that I was on a flat section of the hill where two ridges came together. From here, another ridge went off to the right. Now, I wasn't sure which ridge I had come out.

I looked at the sky for a sign of the sun. The snow fluttered gently down in big flakes, but there was no sun.

Don't panic, I said to myself. Just try to figure things out.

"Not a trace," said my dad's voice. "Not a trace!"

I took a deep breath and fought back the panic. I studied the trees, the ridges, and the steep slopes. In my mind I re-enacted the back-tracking. Finally I stood facing the ridge that went to the left. Right now the only thing that I was absolutely sure of was that I had come out that ridge.

I started back along the ridge toward what I thought was home. I didn't know it at the time, but I was actually headed deeper onto Disappearance Ridge.

Now it was snowing very hard. The large flakes poured down through the bare trees, quickly covering the ground. I was glad I had listened to Grampa and brought the hat. I'm sure it looked silly, but it kept the snow off my hair and out of my eyes.

I trudged on. The ground was covered. In no time, the snow was at least an inch deep and more poured from the sky. I stopped to search the horizon, but it was only a white mist. I kept fighting panic.

Up ahead I saw a large pine tree. It was unusual for a pine tree to grow alone in this area, but there it was, looking like a giant Christmas tree, decorated with snow. The tree seemed warm and inviting, so I headed toward its shelter. Maybe I'd take a few minutes to try to collect my bearings.

I walked under the low limbs of the tree and shook off the snow. I was almost completely protected under the canopy of limbs. I took a deep breath and searched the horizon again. White mist.

I brushed the snow from my jacket and shook it from my hat. I looked around at the ground and was amazed at how deep the snow had become in such a short time. Suddenly my eye caught something on the ground just inside the canopy of limbs. In the light dusting of snow that had blown under the edge of the tree was a lone footprint. I felt the panic rising as I stared at the footprint. I remembered hearing that one of the things that happens to you when you're lost in the woods is that you tend to walk in circles.

I thought about the time my dad and I got lost over on another ridge about two miles away. We had gone 'coon hunting and had treed, as usual, a 'possum. The truth is that there were no raccoons in this part of West Virginia at the time. Poachers had killed them out of season for so many years that there were none left for sports hunters like dad and me. Of course, when you're poor and unemployed, a legally designated hunting season comes second to feeding your hungry children.

Dad and I shook the 'possum out of the tree and headed back to the car. Dad led the way and the dog trailed along, sniffing around for the scent of other animals. After a while we realized we were lost in the darkness. We tried a number of alternate routes; we listened for sounds that might tell us which was the right direction, but all to no avail. Finally Dad had the idea of hooking his belt to the dog's collar and telling him to "go home."

The dog seemed to know what to do, just like Lassie. After a while, we began to feel that we were not going in the right direction, but we followed. It was our only hope. Soon the dog stopped, sat, and looked up into a small tree. The dog was "home," but we were confused. After a moment, we realized he had brought us back to where he treed the 'possum. From the tree, we were able to find our way back to the car. But the startling thing is that we had come back around to the tree in a large circle.

Now, I stood, staring at a footprint some ten feet away, a footprint that meant that I was surely lost and walking in a circle.

Evidently, when I passed by here before, I brushed beneath the edge of the tree and left the print in the light snow. It was protected by the tree, while the other prints filled with snow. But why didn't I notice the tree before?

I walked across the open space under the tree to look at the print. Instinctively, I placed my booted foot beside it. It certainly was not *my* footprint. It was much too small for my foot, almost like a child's foot. And it wasn't a boot print. It was more like a soleless shoe, like a moccasin.

A moccasin! The thought sent chills up and down my spine. I took a closer look at the print. It *was* a moccasin, as sure as the world. And I knew whose moccasin it was. It belonged to "Little Joey" Ramsey who, three years ago, killed his brother and then vanished on Disappearance Ridge without a trace.

I first met "Little Joey" the day after my tenth birthday. He had the most striking golden blond hair I had ever seen, and seemed as happy-go-lucky as any twelve-year-old kid. I learned later that, at the time, he was actually twenty-three years old.

As we stood facing each other in the bright sun, Little Joey, as everyone called him, cocked his head sort of sideways, squinted his left eye closed, and carefully looked me over with his right eye.

"I'm an Indian," he said boldly.

I stood there in my brand-new slightly too big birthday cowboy hat wearing a holster containing a dandy chrome-plated, plastic-ivory handled six shooter cap pistol.

"I'm a cowboy," I told him.

"Good," he said. "Let's play cowboy and Indians."

And we did. All that day.

I had accompanied my Grampa across the hill to a neighbor's farm, the Ramsey's, where he had a day's worth of work cutting hay. It took a lot of pleading, but finally Grampa said I could go until lunchtime if I didn't cause any trouble.

It was a wonderful experience. I got to ride on the horse-drawn mower with its raised sickle bar. I was stationed in front of Grampa and had to hold on for dear life. There were a couple of scary moments when we were going down some rough terrain, but I pretended not to notice.

And of course I was "very good," just like I promised to be. That was because of Little Joey. We liked each other from the start and spent the day at play.

Little Joey was a master at games. We played cowboys and Indians for a while, but mostly we were both Indians. He named me "Redwing" because of my red hair. I called him "Golden Eagle," a name he dearly loved.

Together, Golden Eagle and Redwing tracked the wild buffalo, fought off attacking cavalry, built a tepee, and smoked an imaginary peace pipe. We whooped and rode our "pintos" all day. I was very sad when Grampa called to me and told me it was time to go home.

"Can I come back tomorrow?" I pleaded.

Grampa laughed. "No. We got it all done today."

"Please."

"Richie!" It was my Grampa's firm voice. I knew not to pursue the request.

"Get your stuff," he admonished. "And don't forget your hat."

I'd stopped wearing the hat since, for most of the day I was "Redwing" rather than a cowboy.

Little Joey and I went off to gather up my stuff. We talked sadly, but not saying what we felt in our hearts. Finally, as my Grampa called "for the last time" and started off across the field with the horses and mower, Golden Eagle pulled me aside. We shook hands in a special curled finger, thumb-to-thumb handshake he had taught me. As we did, he suddenly took his knife and made a quick slice across both of our thumbs. I tried to jerk my hand back, but he held tight. I started to cry.

"Shh!" he said. "Look."

I stopped crying and looked at our hands. Our blood ran together in a little pool between our thumbs.

"Redwing is my brother," he whispered.

I stared at him and nodded.

"And Golden Eagle is *my* brother," I responded.

We held our hands together for a brief moment, and then I ran across the field to catch up with Grampa.

That night at the dinner table, I tried to figure out the bits and pieces of a somewhat coded conversation between Grampa and Grandma as they talked about Little Joey. I wasn't sure about most of it, but what it boiled down to had to do with whether Grampa had made a good decision in letting me spend the day playing with my new "Blood Brother."

Finally I asked Grampa if there was something wrong with Little Joey.

"No. Not really." Grampa tried to smooth the situation over, but Grandma was a little more forthright.

"He's tetched in the head, Richie," she told me. "He and his brother got into a fight when Joey was twelve and his brother hurt him real bad. He chopped him right down through the middle of his head with an axe."

"Tish!" Grampa admonished.

"Well, it's true!" she said to Grampa. "Right down the middle. And he's been twelve years old ever since!"

"I didn't see anything," I said.

"It's hardly noticeable." Grampa said, then tried to change the subject. But Grandma had more to say.

"Sneaked up behind him and chopped his skull open. Liked to kilt him. He covers up the scar with that bandanna he wears. And thinks he's an Indian. The boy ought to be in an institution!"

"What's an institution?" I asked.

"It's like a home where they could take care of him." Grampa tried to change the subject again. "How about some pie?"

Grandma got up to get the pie. When she returned, she was calmer.

"Sometimes I feel sorry for the poor boy. But I think the institution might be best. Who's going to look after him now that his mom's dead?"

We ate our pie in silence. Grampa saucered his coffee in his usual way, a way I'd never seen before or since. I asked for some coffee so I could saucer it too, but I was told I was too young for coffee.

Grampa looked tired, but he still had some chores to do. He went out to the barn. I tried to help Grandma clean up.

"Just run along now. I don't need any more broken dishes."

As I was leaving the kitchen, she called to me.

"Just be careful around him. You never know about someone like that."

I nodded and left the room. As I did, I looked at the tiny cut on my thumb. But, I knew in my heart that I did not need to be afraid of Little Joey Ramsey.

My dreams that night were full of Golden Eagle, my brother. We were tracking a very mean outlaw who turned out to be Little Joey's brother. We caught up with him in a barn. He had his back to us. As we sneaked up to capture him, Golden Eagle handed me an axe.

I woke with a start, my heart racing a mile a minute. After I settled down, I lay there wondering what it would be like to be in an institution.

Later in the summer, Grampa and I went back to the Ramsey's for a "second cutting." My Grandma didn't say much to me, but I knew she didn't like the idea one bit.

It was during this trip that I really saw the sad and evil world in which Little Joey was entangled.

"They're talking about putting me in The Institution," Little Joey confided in me. "They keep telling me that I'm not an Indian and that if I keep saying I am, they'll put me in The Institution."

"Is the institution bad?"

"I don't know. I've never been there, but it must be bad. Why else would they want to put me there?"

I thought about it for a moment.

"An' look at this."

He raised his shirt to show some blisters on his stomach. I examined them closely.

"What's that?" I asked.

"Burns."

"Burns?"

"Yeah. He burns me. He says I got to stop saying I'm an Indian. He says I got to get my mind back or it's going to drive him crazy. Then he burns me and asks me if I'm an Indian."

Golden Eagle started to cry. Then his face tightened.

"How can I not say I'm an Indian? I am an Indian. How can I not be one?"

I didn't know what to say. These were issues that were too great for me to comprehend. All I know was that I didn't want Little Joey to go to an institution, no matter how nice it was.

We didn't play much that day. We tried tracking an imaginary elk through the trees to a spring, but our hearts weren't in it. At the spring we scooped water and drank from our hands because that's the way Indians do. Then we settled against some cool rocks.

"You're lucky," Golden Eagle said. "You get to go to school."

Lucky? I began to think that the axe had done more damage than I imagined.

"I'd love to go to school. I'd love to learn more about my people and the old west, and I'd love to go to Arizona and see where my people live."

"Someday we'll go to Arizona together," I assured him.

"Not if I'm in The Institution," he said.

"I won't let them put you in the institution!"

He looked at me for a moment. There was a look of inspiration in his face.

"I know what! If they do put me in The Institution, you can come and get me out. Then we'll head for Arizona."

"Right!" I said.

I never tracked the wild buffalo with Golden Eagle, my brother, again.

After the murder, I read some newspaper accounts about him. One was an interview with the brother's wife, and it was obviously an unsympathetic view of Little Joey.

She told how, after their mother died, his brother had tried to have Little Joey put in an institution. The state decided he didn't need to be institutionalized. There was no reason he couldn't live with his brother and wife on the family farm. A psychiatrist had declared him to be "harmless."

Six months later, after his brother had tried to discipline him for something he had done, Little Joey went into a rage and pushed a knife up under his brother's rib cage into his heart, then ran away onto Disappearance Ridge.

As I read the article, I was sure the discipline had to do with cigarette burns, the knife was the same one that sliced my thumb, and the art of inserting the knife at the right location was based on a theory that "that's the way an Indian would do it."

The sheriff and other law enforcement agencies searched Disappearance Ridge, using blood hounds. After several weeks of intense searching, Little Joey Ramsey was added to the growing list of those who had vanished on Disappearance Ridge – without a trace.

Of course, the newspaper reporter did not come to question me about Little Joey, nor the sheriff either. Just Grandma. I pretended that it didn't matter much to me. After all, I hadn't seen him in more than five years. But Grandma did manage to get in an "I told you so."

But I did dream about Little Joey out there on Disappearance Ridge almost every night for a month.

Now, here I stood under a tall pine tree in the middle of Disappearance Ridge, staring at the first trace of Little Joey anyone had seen in three years: his moccasin print. As I looked at the print, I realized that I was also unconsciously rubbing the tiny scar on my thumb where Little Joey had cut me when our blood mingled and we became "true Indian brothers."

I looked up. The snow was two or three inches deep by this time. I couldn't see more than a hundred feet through the trees. The panic I had been fighting for an hour began to take over.

I was this close to Little Joey; maybe he had even seen me. I didn't know what to do. Was he dangerous? Would he know me seven years later? Would he kill me too, to keep me from turning him in to the police? I didn't know. And I didn't want to find out.

What I wanted was the quickest way out of this god-forsaken place. I wanted to be back on the farm, eating supper with Grampa and Grandma. I cursed Ole Barnie for his wayward wanderings and the rotten fence post that was an accessory to his escape.

What to do? What to do?

Then I remembered some advice I read or heard: if you're lost in the mountains, find the nearest stream, then follow it in the direction of its flow and eventually you'd find your way out.

I knew that at the bottom of the hill there would be a stream, and I decided to get there as soon as possible. I also knew that by going down the side of the hill, instead of along the ridge I would be moving perpendicular to the way Little Joey was traveling.

I ran from beneath the tree. I worked my way quickly down the side of the hill. It was a gentle slope at first, but suddenly it became very rocky and steep. In fact, to call the side of the hill "steep" might be a misnomer. It was more in the category of "sheer."

Because it was so steep, I had to move along the side of the hill, sometimes even coming back up a little way to escape a large rock or cliff.

The rocks and leaves were wet and slick. I kept falling and getting up and falling. The stupid hat kept getting in my way. I hated that hat. I hated the blinding snow. I hated everything right now.

Suddenly my feet went out from under me. I landed hard on the ground and slid down the hill over some sharp rocks. I clawed at the ground to keep from plunging over a precipice and stopped just in the nick of time. I fought back tears of anger and frustration as I sat on the cold wet ground trying to decide what to do next. It was stupid for me to try to find my way down the side of this hill in a blinding blizzard. I needed another plan.

I looked around. About fifty feet to my right and slightly up the side of the hill was a rock cliff. The top stuck out a little, so it looked like good protection from the snow, a place I could wait out the storm and decide what to do next.

I worked my way along the side of the embankment. As I approached the rock formation, I noticed a small opening at the bottom. I hesitated, for fear that some animal might be living under the rock, but right now all

I wanted was shelter from this snow. I decided to take my chances.

I sat with my back to the rock, looking out at the falling snow. I was not quite totally protected under the rock cliff. Occasionally the snow would swirl back along the side of the rock, but at least I wasn't getting pounded by the snow.

I don't know how long I sat there before I became aware of his presence. All I know is that suddenly I knew he was there, living under this rock. For a moment I couldn't get my breath. Finally, I settled down. Without looking at the opening, I spoke.

"How, Golden Eagle."

His head popped out of the hole.

"Redwing! Redwing, my brother. Is it really you?"

"It is."

He crawled out of the hole and sat beside me, squinting his left eye closed and studying me with his right, just as he had done the first time we met.

"I knew you'd come, my brother. But how did you find me?"

"The Great Spirit has directed my path."

"I should have known."

"We thought that you were dead."

"No. I have survived. I know many ways to live in the forest."

"But how did you escape the dogs when they came to hunt for you?"

"It was easy. When they came looking for me here, I simply went back and lived at the farm. The Mean One's squaw left and I had the place to myself. Then, when the search was over, I came back here."

"Golden Eagle is very wise."

"How have you been, my brother?"

"Busy with school activities and helping my grandparents."

"Yes. The great father limps badly."

"Little misses the keen eyes of Golden Eagle."

"Yes. Mostly I go out at night. But your great father's land is so close, I sometimes see him in the day. How is school?"

"Good. I play sports – football, and I study hard. How do you survive? What do you do for food?"

"I find much food in gardens that others do not want. I can store potatoes, and fruits and vegetables almost all winter here in my cave. Plus, I have friends."

Friends! I remembered a boy who attends the same church I do telling me that he once saw his grandmother leave food in the barn. When he asked about it, she laughed and said it was for the ghost of Disappearance Ridge.

"So others know you are here."

"Only a few."

We sat in silence for a moment.

"What brings you to Disappearance Ridge?"

"My grandfather's horse escaped from the pasture."

"The big brown one."

"Yes."

"I have not seen him today, but I will look. More than likely he is in the cornfield on the Franklin Farm. You must have missed a turn back at the forks of the ridge."

"I missed more than one turn. I was trying to get back home."

"Then the Great Spirit did intend for you to find me. You're going in the opposite direction."

I looked at the little boy-man who had managed to survive for more than three years in a virtual wilderness. He seemed happy. But I wondered if he was. And I wondered how he felt about having killed his own brother. I decided to ask.

"Tell me about what happened. Was it as I suspect?"

"It was. Only worse. The Mean One tried to put me in The Institution, but they said 'no.' After that he got very bad. He burned me often and threatened to kill me.

"The day it happened, he had taken my knife away from me and said he was going to cut out my tongue to keep me from saying I was an Indian. I ran. He was chasing me, shouting, 'I'm going to do the job right this time.' The squaw watched from the porch. She cried for him to stop. He turned and yelled at her. When he did, he tripped and fell. He landed on the knife.

"I ran back to him. He rolled over onto his side. He was trying to talk, but couldn't. I pulled out the knife and blood was all over the place. I knew he would die.

"Now there was no one. They would surely put me in The Institution. Then the squaw started screaming that I had killed him, so I ran into the woods."

I thought about the newspaper article. She had witnessed it, been a part of it, but still told the reporter that Little Joey had stabbed her husband.

"She lied about you. She said you stabbed him."

"I know."

"Why do you stay here, living under a rock like an animal?"

He did not speak for a while. I was beginning to regret the harshness of my words. Finally he said:

"As long as I am here, I am free. Indians are meant to be free. Indians are not meant to live in The Institution."

He was silent for a while.

"Even if I could prove I did not kill the Mean One, I have nowhere to live. They will not let me live alone. That can only mean The Institution."

"But, I would help you. You could live with me."

He thought about what I said.

"Redwing, you are truly my brother. But our ways are different. You have been to school. You know the white man's ways. You will succeed in the white man's world. But I am only an Indian. I must live here. I must be free."

We sat in silence, watching the snow fall. Darkness was settling across the valley.

"I have to get you back to the farm," he said. "The great father and his squaw will be worried."

"Yes."

We rose. I followed Golden Eagle as he picked his way along unseen paths. He walked with ease as I stumbled up the side of the hill. On top of the ridge, we moved quickly back along the way I had come. When we passed the pine tree, I told him of the footprint.

"Yes. I must be more careful. You were at my door before I even knew you were in the woods."

"Perhaps Golden Eagle has been a good teacher to the young warrior Redwing."

He smiled.

"Perhaps."

He turned and started through the brush and trees.

"Follow me closely. Move as I move. That way the limbs will not hit your face."

We moved along swiftly in the now almost dark forest. I tried to locate the two ridges and look for other landmarks, but I did not see them. All the time, I felt I was going in the wrong direction, but suddenly, there in the distance was the farmhouse. I was almost home.

Golden Eagle stood in the shadows.

"The great father will be looking for you. We want him to see only one person."

I turned to Golden Eagle and took his hand in the same way he had clasp mine on that summer day now almost eight years ago. We both looked at the little scars on our thumbs.

"Our blood does not mingle today," I said, "because we are already brothers."

"Yes. And we will always be brothers. Thank you for coming. I hoped you would."

"Oh Golden Eagle," I said, kneeling down in front of him. We were now at about the same height. Tears streamed down my cheeks as I pleaded: "Don't stay here. Come back with me. I'll not let them put you in the institution."

A look of sadness came over his face. He shook his head.

"Redwing, my brother. My home is here."

"Then can I come back here to visit you."

"It would be wonderful to see my brother, to talk, to track the mighty buffalo. But if you come, others will follow. Then I will be captured and put in The Institution."

"Then I will stay away, until the Great Spirit again leads me to your door."

"I look forward to that day."

We remained silent, him standing and me kneeling in front of him. Finally I took off the cowboy hat and placed it on his head. It fit perfectly.

"Keep this to remember me by."

I stood, but I could not leave him there. I just couldn't make myself go. After a moment he spoke.

"Among the white man, Redwing is a very brave warrior. After all, you are one of the few who went to Disappearance Ridge and returned."

He smiled, turned, and vanished into the darkness.

That summer I went to a used book store in Charleston and bought as many books as I could find on Indians and on the Old West. I even bought some fiction books about cowboys and Indians. I put the books into a plastic feed sack and took them as deeply onto Disappearance Ridge as I dared to go. I tied them to a tree limb and left them dangling. I knew he would find them.

I dreamed about Golden Eagle a lot that summer and thought of him often over the years. There were many, many reminders: little kids with golden hair, a trip to Arizona, pictures in magazines, visits to my grandparent's farm, you name it. But, over the last several years, I have not thought of him as often.

Now, almost three decades since I last saw him, I sat staring at a child's cowboy hat, trying to decide what to do next. I wondered what the Sheriff of Kanawha County knew about me and about this hat, and about a little Indian known as Golden Eagle.

As I considered all my options, I finally decided to look into the "windows of the soul" of the Sheriff of Kanawha County to see what they told me about him. They said he was a man to be trusted.

"I remember this hat," I said. "And I remember very well the last time I saw it."

I told him the whole story.

He listened intently, hanging onto every word. He never interrupted, but occasionally he would interject a comment, mostly expletives like: "Well, I'll be damned."

When I was finished, he sat for a few moments in stunned silence. I couldn't tell whether he believed me or not.

"I remember something about that incident," he finally said. "We did a follow-up on it just after I went to work here. I had forgotten all about it."

He stood up and looked at his watch.

"You busy?"

"Not really."

"Got time to come with me? I've got an errand to run and I want to talk to you some more about this Golden Eagle person."

"Sure." After all, I thought, if I don't go, he can always arrest me.

As we walked from his office, Bob picked up his hat and turned to the deputy.

"Susan. I've got a job for you."

"Great."

"About . . . ." He turned to me. "How many years?"

"Uh, twenty-seven, twenty-eight."

"About twenty-seven or twenty-eight years ago, out on Dutch Ridge, a fellow murdered his brother. It was a stabbing. See if you can find a file on it. We were out there. Had some dogs out there."

She looked up from the notes she was making. "Any more to go on?"

Bob shrugged and looked at me.

"Ramsey," I said. "Little Joey Ramsey."

"Right." He turned to her. "The perpetrator was a Joseph Ramsey." Then he turned back to me. "What was the brother's name?"

"The Mean One," I said.

Bob laughed. "I imagine we got a lot of files under that name."

"I don't think I ever knew his brother's name," I said. "Wait! Let me think. Johnny or Jimmy or something like that. It had the same initial as Joey."

Bob turned to the deputy. "Got that?"

"Got it."

"I'll be back in an hour. Have the file on my desk."

She smiled. "Yes sir, Sir."

"Great staff," he said to me as we headed for the door. Although he said it to me, it was certainly loud enough to be heard by everyone in the room. And I'm sure that was what Bob intended.

Bob was silent as we rode. I listened to the police dispatcher on the scanner. We pulled up into the driveway of a large building. I looked for a sign. "Charleston Medical Center," it read.

Bob parked in a space that said "For Emergency Vehicles Only," picked up his cellular telephone, and got out. I followed. We walked quickly to the entrance and through the doors.

"Hey, Ed," Bob said to the security person behind the desk.

"Hey Sheriff," Ed answered.

We strode past.

"Retired from the Charleston Police," Bob told me as we turned the corner and headed down a corridor. I followed Bob as he bounded up a flight of stairs, into another corridor, and through a set of large double doors. Immediately, we were at a nurses' station that seemed to block entry to the ward. Three nurses were working the station. They all looked up quickly. When they saw Bob, they smiled.

"Dr. Robenski in?" Bob asked.

"In her office," said the head nurse.

We didn't break stride as we turned down the corridor. I was practically running to keep up.

We stopped at the open door of an office. Bob tapped on the door, then leaned inside.

"Hello Doc."

"Howdy, Sheriff," came a voice from inside. Even with the attempt at imitation, it was obviously not a West Virginia voice.

"Got a minute?"

"I always got time fer the Sher'f of Kanawha County."

"Good! Grab your keys."

Dr. Robenski came out of her office and we continued our foot race down the corridor. As we did, I noticed the name and title beside her door. Dr. Robenski was head of the hospital's psychiatric ward.

We were walking swiftly down the hall when Bob turned to Dr. Robenski and said: "Oh, I forgot to introduce you. Dr. Robenski, this is 'Redwing.'"

She stopped so abruptly that I almost ran into her. She turned and looked at my hair and beard.

"Yes. Of course," she said. "Nice to meet you, Mr. Redwing."

"Just 'Redwing,'" Bob corrected.

"Where did you find him?" Dr. Robenski asked Bob.

"Old school chum. We played football together."

"How interesting."

Then we started back down the hall.

We stopped in front of the door to one of the rooms. The door was closed. Dr. Robenski looked at me, then at Bob. Bob nodded. She took a key and unlocked the door. I stood, waiting for them to go in. Bob nodded to me, and then gestured for me to enter. I stepped into the doorway and stopped.

At first glance, the room looked like an ordinary hospital room except that the covers had been removed from the bed and tied together to form a tent-like space. And there, in front of the tent, seated on a small rug, was Golden Eagle.

He was staring at the floor. He didn't look up or do anything else that would indicate that he was aware of our presence. His golden blond hair was now snow white and his skin was tanned a deep brown. Otherwise, he still looked like a twelve-year-old child.

Bob took my arm and pulled me back from the door. He nodded to Dr. Robenski, who closed the door.

"Last fall, some hunters got a little inebriated and decided to see if there were any deer on Disappearance Ridge. Just after they got out on the Ridge, one of the hunters said he heard something. The others thought he was just spoofing them, but then they all heard it. They said it sounded for sure like a child coughing. They claim they looked around for the source of the cough, but more likely, they sobered up quick and made a rather hasty retreat out of there."

We smiled as we thought about the frightened hunters.

"One of the hunters knows my deputy, Doug Holt, and told him about it. We pretty much dismissed it as a figment of their drunken imaginations, but they swore it was true and offered to take Doug back out there. Doug and one of the hunter's went, but they didn't find anything and they didn't hear anything.

"Doug's from up at Sanderson and for some reason he kept thinking about the cough. I guess he really believed his buddy. So, early this spring, he took his day off and went out there and walked around the woods. He got lost, of course, but he did hear the cough.

"Well, he took several other deputies and they went back the next day and searched the area. It took them all day, but they finally found him in a cave under a rock cliff. The opening was so small that they had to go and get shovels to dig him out. By the time we got him here, he was nearly dead. He had the worst case of pneumonia the medical staff had ever seen and how he lived through it, no one knows."

Bob paused and looked at Dr. Robenski.

"He's been pretty cooperative lately, but at first he fought like a wild cat."

"I'll never forget," Dr. Robenski said thoughtfully. "Three nurses were holding him down while I administered a shot. I thought we'd never be able to hold him. But, after a few minutes, he stopped fighting. He squinted his left eye closed and studied me carefully with his right eye. I thought he was about to say something, but he didn't. He just turned his head away and big tears rolled down his cheeks.

After that, he seemed resigned to whatever we wanted to do."

"But he's never talked!" added Bob. "We didn't even know if he could talk. He's been here since May and never said one single word."

"How is he?" I asked.

"Fine," Dr. Robenski said. "Physically, he's in good condition. We know nothing about his mental state. After we moved him to this room, he took the covers off the bed and made that tent. We have determined some of the foods he likes and we make sure he gets plenty to eat. But, for the most part, he refuses to acknowledge that we exist."

"Can I talk to him?"

"Oh, yes. Please."

Dr. Robenski opened the door. I took a deep breath, walked in, and sat beside Golden Eagle on the floor. He did not look up. I waited a minute or two to see what he would do. If he was aware that I was in the room, he didn't show it.

"Golden Eagle," I whispered.

For a moment I was afraid he hadn't heard me, but then he turned his face to mine.

"Oh, Redwing," he said softly. "Is it really you?"

"It is."

"I have prayed that you would come."

"The Great Spirit has heard your prayers."

He turned his face back to the floor. "Oh, Redwing. I am sad that you find me here, in this place."

"In this place?"

"Yes. The Institution."

"No," I told him. "This is not The Institution."

"It isn't?"

"No, this is only The Hospital. You were very sick."

"Yes. My chest burned like fire. I thought I would die."

"It is good that they found you and brought you to The Hospital."

"And it is good that you have come, but how did you know I was here?"

"The Captain of the soldiers is a friend of mine," I said, gesturing toward Bob. Golden Eagle looked toward the door.

"He is a great warrior?"

"Yes. And he wishes to be a friend of Golden Eagle."

Golden Eagle looked back toward the door, squinting his left eye closed to study the Sheriff. I motioned for Bob to join us. He came and agilely assumed a cross-legged position on the floor beside us.

"Captain, this is my friend and brother, Chief Golden Eagle."

"I am happy to meet you," Bob said.

"Chief Golden Eagle wishes to thank you and your soldiers for saving his life," I said.

Golden Eagle looked at me for a moment as if to say "I do?" Then he looked at Bob and nodded.

"We were happy to be of service."

"The Chief has been concerned that he was in The Institution."

"No," Bob said to Golden Eagle. "This is a hospital."

Golden Eagle studied the floor for a moment, then turned to me. "Then why does the Captain keep the door locked?"

There was a moment of silence while my mind raced for an answer.

"May I remind my brother," I said quickly, "that Golden Eagle has not always cooperated with the Captain or the Medicine Man." I gestured to Dr. Robenski. "The Captain feared Golden Eagle's enemies might come and try to attack him."

Golden Eagle seemed pleased to think he was being protected. He smiled at Bob who smiled at Golden Eagle and then at me.

"Golden Eagle thanks the Captain of the soldiers," Golden Eagle said, "but please remember that Golden Eagle has much strength and can protect himself very well."

Bob nodded. "I am aware of that now. But then, you were very weak."

"Yes I was."

There was a moment of silence.

"Golden Eagle is now worried about the length of his stay," I said. "He does not wish to burden the hospital."

"Golden Eagle is no burden. We would like for him to stay as long as possible."

"Perhaps we should talk with the Medicine Man about this." I gestured to Dr. Robenski. She came over and joined our pow-wow.

Golden Eagle squinted the left eye shut and looked at Dr. Robenski. "She has inflicted much pain on Golden Eagle's bottom," he said, rubbing his hip. "But I know that she is very kind. I have heard her called Robenski, which in my language means 'One Who Heals.'"

Dr. Robenski smiled. "Golden Eagle needs to remain here at the hospital for only a little longer," she said, speaking directly to Golden Eagle. "He is still frail from the illness. But, now that he knows he is among friends, I feel he will improve much faster."

We all agreed that Dr. Robenski was right.

"But I do feel that Golden Eagle needs to get out of this room and go for a walk, beginning right now," she added.

Golden Eagle's face lit up. "Do you mean it?"

"I certainly do. I'll personally give you a guided tour of the hospital."

Golden Eagle leaped to his feet. "Oh, Redwing. Things always work out better when you are around."

We stood.

"I'll be back to see you tomorrow," I told him. He extended his hand and we shook hands; fingers curled, thumb-to-thumb. He gently touched the scar on my thumb and looked up into my face.

"Could you bring me some more books?" he asked.

"I sure can."

Golden Eagle said goodbye to Bob and me and followed Dr. Robenski through the door.

For several seconds, Bob and I stood in silence, looking toward the open door. It was one of those times when you feel that you need to say something profound, but you just don't know what to say. Finally, Bob said it: "Well, I'll be dagnabbed if this ain't the darn'dest thing I ever saw."

As we walked by the nurses' station on our way out, Golden Eagle was the center of attention.

When we arrived back at Bob's office, the deputy handed him the file he had asked for. He took it with him into his office.

"Come on in," he told her.

He sat at his desk and studied the contents of the file for quite a while. Then he handed it to the deputy.

"Put it back," he told her. "I think we'll just consider this case forever unresolved."

"Good call," she said. She took the file and left. As she did, I noticed the cowboy hat. I had left it on Bob's desk.

"Can we return the hat to Golden Eagle?" I asked.

"Certainly. I'll drop it off this evening."

Bob gestured toward the chair.

"Nah. I really should go," I said. "That is, if I'm free to go."

He laughed. I stood there for a moment, then asked. "What will happen to him?"

Bob leaned back in his chair. The thought seemed to trouble him.

"I've been wonderin' that myself. I'll have to talk to Dr. Robenski, but I been thinking about seeing if my folks will let him stay with them. They've got a big farm and he'd have plenty of privacy. Besides, with all their grandchildren and great-grandchildren, there'd be lots of kids his age to play with."

Bob stopped to think about what he had just said. He smiled for a moment, then the smile turned to a frown.

"Another thing. Your sister works for the newspaper, right?"

"Works for the newspaper! Without her, there'd be no newspaper," I joked. But I could tell Bob was not in a joking mood.

"Well, I've kept this thing pretty close. I've sworn all my people to secrecy and the hospital's people too. If the press gets a hold of this, they'll turn it into a circus."

"Don't worry. Diane's not on the news side. She just makes sure that the computers work. Besides, I can keep a secret."

"Good!"

"Before I go, answer one question for me."

"What's that?"

"Well, what stroke of luck or great investigative powers led you to connect me with Golden Eagle? And how did you make the association between me and Redwing?"

He picked up the hat and handed it to me.

"The hat?" I said. "I figured that. But how did you know it was *my* hat?"

"I jus' read the hat band."

"The hat band?"

I turned the hat over and looked inside. There on the band, in childish block letters, I had written my name: "Richie Smith." And beside my name, Golden Eagle had used his knife to scratch the words "Redwing is my brother."

The Moonshine Man

32 And there were also two other,
malefactors, led with him to be put to death.

33 And when they were come to the
place, which is called Calvary, there they
crucified him, and the malefactors, one on the
right hand, and the other on the left.

39 And one of the malefactors which
were hanged railed on him, saying, If thou be
Christ, save thyself and us.

40 But the other answering rebuked
him, saying, Dost not thou fear God, seeing
thou art in the same condemnation?

41 And we indeed justly; for we receive
the due reward of our deeds: but this man
hath done nothing amiss.

42 And he said unto Jesus, Lord,
remember me when thou comest into thy
kingdom.

43 And Jesus said unto him, Verily I say unto thee, To day shalt thou be with me in paradise.

Luke 23: 32 - 33; 39 - 43
King James Version

WE CALLED HIM "The Moonshine Man." Not because he made and sold moonshine, but because he used to. During the 1920's, 30's, and 40's, the Moonshine Man ran a still somewhere so deep in the rugged terrain between Sanderson and Dutch Ridge that no one ever knew where it was. The Revenuers knew about it, but, try as they might, they just couldn't find it.

Everyone from Pinch to Pond Gap was curious about where it might be, but in truth, no one really wanted to find it, even accidentally. My dad and I talked about the still occasionally when we would go night hunting on Dutch Ridge, but we purposefully avoided hunting in the area where most people thought it was. And, Uncle Ron and I talked bravely about it when we were teenagers. We made plans to search the area for as long as it took to find it. But, it seems, we never had a good opportunity to put our plan into action.

During Prohibition, the Moonshine Man was a major distributor of alcoholic beverage to a number of establishments in the Charleston area. It was a family affair. The Moonshine

Man and his brothers ran the still, beginning when they were quite young.

But Repeal brought changes and the still could no longer support the Moonshine Man and his brothers, so the brothers found other work, while the Moonshine Man continued to ply his trade.

In 1944, the Moonshine Man's only son, who was 18 years old at the time, was hauling a load to Charleston when he was intercepted by the law. Someone had tipped them that he would be making a run on a Friday night, and they were waiting. There was a confrontation, but the law had planned well, or so they thought. As the son sped through a roadblock, they opened fire. When the smoke cleared, the Moonshine Man's son was in custody, and a Deputy Sheriff was dead, shot twice in the chest.

Although the son claimed he didn't have a gun, he was charged with killing the deputy, convicted of first degree murder, and sentenced to be executed.

The whole affair was so traumatic for the Moonshine Man that he abandoned his mash barrels and never distilled another drop.

During WWII, while my dad was in the Navy, my mother, bother, and I lived in a small house in Quick, West Virginia. But when dad came home, we moved to Elk Two Mile and I attended first grade there. Then, at the end of the school year, Mom and Dad bought an old run down four-room house in Quick and we moved back. The house was a somewhat dilapidated mining shack. It had gas for heating and electricity for lights. But, it had no running water or indoor plumbing, a deficiency that Mom soon remedied by having an addition built that included a kitchen and bathroom.

It was about the time that we moved back to Quick, after school was out for the summer but before my seventh birthday in July, when I spent a week or two with my mom's parents, Grampa and Gramma Kennedy. They lived in a four-room house about a mile from Sanderson that was affectionately known as "the old house." It had no gas, electricity, or running water. Cooking and heating were done with wood and coal stoves; water was carried from the spring; kerosene lamps were used for lighting; and the bathroom was "out back." By almost any standard, we were deprived. But then, so was everyone else we knew.

While I was visiting, we ate supper later in the evening, usually at dark, because my grandfather worked long days recapping tires for Goodyear Tire and Rubber, then did farm chores till dusk. To keep us kids from getting too hungry, Gramma would feed us a snack at about four or five o'clock. It was usually brown beans with juice soaked into cold biscuits or leftover cornbread, and was considered a delicacy.

One night, as we prepared to eat supper and just as Gramma finished "asking the blessing," there was a knock on the front door. A knock at the front door meant the person was a stranger. Had it been family or friends, they would have walked right in. And, they would have come to the back door. Only company and strangers came to the front door.

Gramma looked at Grampa, then got up and went to see who was at the door. We heard soft talking from the porch. That meant, strangely, whoever it was didn't want to come in the house. In a moment, Gramma returned. She looked at Grampa, an expression of distress on her face. Without a word, he got up and left the room. We heard the front door close, so we couldn't hear Grampa's conversation from the porch.

We questioned Gramma about who was at the door. At first, she ignored our questions and told us "Eat your supper." But, we wanted to know and kept asking. Finally, with an uncharacteristic flash of anger, she said that we should "shut up and eat!" For us, this was a signal that Gramma did not want to talk about who was at the door and continued questions would only bring a calamity none of us wanted. So, we shut up and ate.

After what seemed like a long time, Grampa came back to the table. He sat down, then glanced at Gramma. She gave him a look of concern. He – and we – finished supper in silence.

After supper, while we did our chores and helped Gramma with the dishes, Grampa left. He told Gramma that he had to talk with his brothers about something important. Since he walked to where they lived, we knew he would be talking with Carl and Harley, both of whom lived nearby, on the other side of Blue Creek.

Grampa's sudden disappearance was a great disappointment for us, because he had promised to tell us ghost stories. It was a ritual. Once or twice a week, Grampa would dim the kerosene lamps, gather us around, and tell ghost stories. We had heard the stories before and would hear them many times again. Every time he told them, he assured us that the stories were true and, in fact, had happened to him, or someone he knew. It was an exciting time and when the "gotcha" line came at the end, we'd scream and huddle close to him. Huddling, hugging, and howling was a favorite past time for us and for Grampa.

But, tonight we went to bed before Grampa returned, disappointed that there were no stories.

The next night, a similar incident occurred. The knock came just at dark. This time, Grampa got up, went through the living room to the front door, and stepped outside to talk to the visitor.

Grampa was not gone long. When he returned, he glanced at Gramma who looked away. Again we ate in silence, and again there were no stories. Even though Grampa was home, he was not in the mood.

Whatever was going on between Grampa and this mysterious visitor was serious and secretive for reasons which young children were not supposed to know. So, we didn't ask, but we kept our ears open for clues. We gathered from the few clues we had that the visitor was a man and that he had asked Grampa for a favor and that Grampa had to get an okay from his brothers. From the porch on the second nightly visit, we heard in low tones Grampa say something like "not in the main area, outside the fence," and to Gramma's query as of who would help, he had said "Cricket (that's my dad), Kester (my oldest uncle), and Harley."

That was about it, except for the distinct impression that Gramma was dead set against whatever was going to take place. According to her, it was a "disgrace" and "don't ever put me in there with him!"

The next day was Saturday. It was usually a busy day for Grampa. He worked at Goodyear half a day and then, when he got home, he would dig coal from a small mine near the house, plow, mend roofs and fences, and do other chores. But today, he didn't go to work. Instead he got up early and went down to the building called the "chicken coop," which, in my memory had never housed a chicken, rummaged around until he found a pick and shovel, then started walking across a field toward the swinging bridge. Dave, Ron, and I ran to catch up with him.

"Can we go?"

"No," he said. "This is a big job and you'd only get in the way."

"We can dig."

He stopped and looked at us. He was obviously in no mood to discuss what he was going to do and why we could not go.

"I'll tell you what. Tonight, we'll tell stories and maybe Edith will make fudge or something."

That satisfied Ron and me, and we ran back toward the house. But David stayed to argue. He was four years older than us – Ron and I were the same age, only two months apart. After a while, David came back to the house. He was mad because he couldn't go and started teasing us, so we'd be mad too.

Around noon, Grampa came back. He was covered with dirt and needed a bath. So, he got soap and went down to the creek to bathe. We wanted to join him, but he said no. So, we stood on the bank and threw rocks and sticks in the creek.

When he came back to the house, he went into the bedroom to change clothes. Gramma went in with him and closed the door. We listened carefully to the muffled voices, but couldn't tell what was being said. Finally, the door opened and Gramma came out in a huff.

"We're going and that's that." She said over her shoulder. She grabbed a pair of scissors and went outside. We felt it best not to join her and watched from a distance as she went about selecting blooms from her flower garden, the rose bushes, and the other flowers she had planted around the yard.

She arranged the flowers in a bouquet and told us "get straightened up. We're going." We didn't know where, but we assumed that when we got there we'd solve the mystery of the man who came knocking. And, we knew it was a formal affair, like church, because we had to comb our hair.

Grampa, Gramma (with flowers), and the three of us boys, walked down the road to the creek and crossed the swinging bridge. The swinging bridge was always exciting. It was about ten feet high and bounced with each step. There was a cadence to crossing the bridge, and if you got out of step, it felt like the bridge would hurl you into the water.

And, you didn't look down at the creek through the cracks. Otherwise, you'd "freeze" and someone would have to come lead you off the bridge. You didn't want that to happen because you'd be teased about it for the rest of your life.

As usual, David tried to scare us by bouncing the bridge. We whined to Gramma, but she just looked at us and admonished us to "get on across." On the other side, we walked the path to the road, then turned toward Harley's place. But, we knew we weren't going to Harley's. To go to his place, we walked the railroad tracks and went through the cut in the hill that had once been a tunnel until it collapsed.

Instead, we walked down the road, toward the Kennedy Family Cemetery. And when we got to the cemetery, we discovered that it was our destination. There, just outside the fence, was a new grave. And there, waiting, was the Moonshine Man. When we approached, he nodded gravely toward my Gramma, who nodded back.

In about ten minutes, a car drove up. It was my dad and Uncle Kester. A few minutes later, Harley came walking up the road. Everyone nodded, but no one spoke. It seemed a little more grim than most funerals I'd been to, but I didn't know why.

We stood in the road and waited.

After a while, the Moonshine Man looked at his watch. "They said two o'clock," he said to no one in particular. I didn't know what time it was, but I guessed that whoever said two o'clock was late.

A half hour passed. Gramma kept an eye on us, so we were on our best behavior. But it was getting harder and harder not to chase each other, or throw rocks, or something. Then, a truck came up the road. It was a panel truck, so I thought it would pass. But it stopped. On the door was the West Virginia State Seal. A man got out and talked with the Moonshine Man. After a few minutes, the Moonshine Man called to my grandfather.

"He says I have to read and sign this," the Moonshine Man said to Grampa, "but I can't read."

The man from the truck handed the paper to Grampa who quietly read it to the

Moonshine Man. The Moonshine Man nodded as Grampa read. When the reading was finished, Grampa showed the Moonshine Man where to mark an X on the paper. Grampa then signed below the X.

The man opened the back doors of the panel truck. Dad, Kester, Harley, Grampa, and the Moonshine Man, came around the truck, carrying a box. I had expected a casket, but, although it was the right size, it was just a plain wooden box.

The men carried the box past us toward the grave. We followed. The box was placed by the grave on some ropes. The men then lifted the ropes, raised the box, and lowered it into the ground.

Everyone stood silently, looking into the grave. I wondered where the preacher was. There was always a preacher. I started to ask Gramma, but just then, the Moonshine Man looked toward her. On his face was a sad, pleading look, and his eyes had a message for Gramma. She nodded, stepped closer to the grave, and said a prayer. She prayed about life, death, the resurrection, heaven, the forgiveness of sin, and the thief on the cross.

When the prayer was over, the men picked up shovels and began to fill the grave. This was usually our signal to leave, but this time we stayed. When the grave was filled and the mound soothed, Gramma gently placed the flowers on the fresh dirt. The Moonshine Man picked up a crude homemade wooden cross with a name carved on it and pushed the sharpened point into the soft ground at the head of the grave.

We stood quietly until the Moonshine Man began to walk away. We followed. But when he had only taken a few steps, the Moonshine Man stopped, turned, and looked back at the grave. Suddenly, he began to cry. Not just quietly, but in loud sobs. The men walked back to where he was and stood beside him. Had there not been a taboo in our family for men to touch, someone would probably have put an arm around his shoulder.

Robby

21 Ye have heard that it was said by them of old time, Thou shalt not kill; and whosoever shall kill shall be in danger of the judgment:

22 But I say unto you, That whosoever is angry with his brother without a cause shall be in danger of the judgment: and whosoever shall say to his brother, Raca, shall be in danger of the council: but whosoever shall say, Thou fool, shall be in danger of hell fire.

23 Therefore if thou bring thy gift to the altar, and there rememberest that thy brother hath ought against thee;

24 Leave there thy gift before the altar, and go thy way; first be reconciled to thy brother, and then come and offer thy gift.

Matthew 5:21 - 24
King James Version

I TALKED TO Mom and Dad last night and they said that they had been to Charleston, to the Mall, and had seen Robby Robinson, and that Robby had said to tell me hello and that he'd like to see me the next time I'm home.

It's been a while since I've seen Robby. In fact, I guess I've only talked to him a half dozen times since the incident that took place on Sanderson Days when I thought we were going to get into a lot more trouble than we ever did when we were growing up as kids.

Although I claim to be from Quick, Sanderson is the official town of my birth. The truth is that I was born "near Sanderson," in a house that everyone called "the old house." It was located at the foot of a small knoll known as "Tater Knob." But we didn't want to seem "uppity," so on my birth certificate, they put that I was born at Sanderson.

The incident involving Robby and me, to which I referred, took place at the Sanderson Day Celebration on July 4, 1972. Sanderson Day was held every Fourth of July for more than fifty years. But now everyone has moved away, and they pretty much closed the town. Today there are a few houses left in what was once a thriving sawmill and coal mining town with a population of 500 or more. I don't remember either the sawmill or the coal mines, but I remember Sanderson, although the Sanderson I knew was a much smaller version of the town in its heyday.

In 1972, I was visiting my parents during early July and thought I'd go to Sanderson Days just to see if anyone was there that I knew. I asked Mom and Dad if they wanted to go along, but they didn't, so I went alone.

The town had dwindled a lot since I was there last, some ten years before. Sanderson only had one real road. It ran right through the middle of the town, going from west to east. As far as I can remember, it had never been paved. The road dead-ended on the eastern edge of town. That was as far as you could go. So, in more ways than one, Sanderson was a "dead-end" town.

The railroad ran through Sanderson, paralleling the car road, and continued another 15 or 20 miles on up to the head of the line. The railroad's red brick depot was mid-way between the east and west ends of town. In 1972, it had been closed a long time, but the building still stood, a monument to the better and more prosperous days Sanderson knew until the end of World War Two.

With few exceptions, the "better" homes were on the south side of the railroad. The small four room hastily built houses known as "coal mining shacks" were on the north side, giving full meaning to the expression of "being from the wrong side of the tracks."

As I mingled among the small crowd that had gathered for Sanderson Days, I met a few people I remembered and a few more who remembered me. We were all under the big dark grey tent. In the past, the tent would have housed only a small percentage of the crowd and the din would have been deafening.

The tent, with its rolled up flaps to allow the breeze through on this very warm day, brought back a lot of memories of the tent revivals that were held in Sanderson when I was a very young kid. They lasted two weeks or more and if you were a "good" Christian, you never missed a night. The services were very different from anything I've seen since. There was a lot of very upbeat music and singing. Then, after an offering was taken, of course, the preacher spent the better part of an hour trying to scare the hell out of us (literally, not figuratively).

I was talking to Aunt Pansy about one such revival when I noticed that a hush had fallen over the crowd. Pansy had become distracted and was looking past me at something down the road. I turned to see what she and everyone else was staring at. It was a car. Actually, it was a Volkswagen bus, a very odd looking Volkswagen bus painted with designs that fit the era. "Love" and "Peace" were painted in large letters and there was a large peace symbol painted on the nose. I glanced at the bus and thought nothing much of it. I'd seen lots of those brightly painted fixtures of the current age in Kansas City, where I was living at the time. But then, I remembered that this was

Sanderson, West Virginia, and such a spectacle might not be so common.

The Volkswagen bus got closer, chugged to a stop, the door opened, and out climbed Robby Robinson. Robby's clothing was most appropriate for the early 1970s and his hair and beard were very long. He looked the part of a somewhat older Hippie, which, at 30, he was.

I was delighted to see him, and quickly started in his direction. But, as I moved through the crowd, I began to realize that I was probably the only person there who was glad to see Robby.

As I greeted him with a warm handshake, I could tell that he was glad to see me too. We chatted briefly and then came inside the tent. As Robby walked through the crowd, several people greeted him, none warmly. But, for a few people, saying hello was the proper thing to do. After all, he was born in Sanderson, and downtown Sanderson at that, not some outlying area like Tater Knob. He grew up in Sanderson. And, everyone remembered his dad and mom, and his brother David. In fact, a lot of people in the tent were kin to him.

Robby and I got something to drink and found a place to sit, along the edge of the tent, where we could talk. We were absorbed in conversation, remembering old times in Sanderson, when I heard Robby say "Uh-oh."

I turned to see what had caused him to say "Uh-oh," and there, coming toward us, was about half a dozen young all-American boys. I could tell by the look on their faces that trouble was brewing and that Robby was the object of their anger. I looked at Robby. He didn't seem to be overly concerned. I'm sure this was not the first confrontation with an angry crowd that he'd faced. His had been a long career of confrontations and to him, this was just another one. To me, it was a bit frightening. After all, I reasoned, whatever they did unto him, they might do unto me also.

Robby glanced at me and smiled.

"I'll handle it," he said in a low voice.

When the boys reached our table, every eye in the place was looking in our direction. I heard a woman's voice say "somebody do something," but nobody moved. The group stood crossed armed, staring at Robby. They seemed not to notice me, which did not upset me too badly. After a moment, the leader of the group, and the biggest of the bunch, leaned forward, placed his knuckles on the table and spoke to Robby.

"You don't belong here, Maggot," he said. "We want you and your redheaded buddy to get out of Sanderson before we kick your pink-o commie butts all the way back to California."

So, they had noticed me after all. That meant, if there was going to be trouble, I was going to be in the middle of it. But, this wouldn't be the first time that Robby and I had stood together in a showdown with bullies. Robby and I had grown up together and had been special friends from the time were very young.

Robby was a year or two younger than me. He was Charlie and Marjorie Robinson's son, one of their two children, both boys. Charlie was Sanderson's most affluent and influential citizen. He owned the store, had some houses that he rented, and dabbled in other local business ventures. Robby and I were cousins. His dad was my Aunt Harriette's brother. I should say, one of her brothers since there were eleven kids in her family. Aunt Harriette was actually my great-aunt, my great-grandmother's sister. So that made Robby fourth or fifth or sixth cousin. Even more than cousins, we were pals.

Before the Quick Church of the Nazarene was organized, my family (Mom, all of us kids, my mom's parents, and assorted aunts and uncles) attended the community church in Sanderson. It was a "Holiness" church with "Wesleyan tendencies," but was not associated with any denomination. To say the least, it was conservative in its religious beliefs and practices.

Almost every Sunday when I was growing up, I spent the day with Robby. We'd play all day and then I'd go home after church Sunday night. Robby and I also attended school together at Quick Elementary School, but Sunday was our time to play together and those Sundays were very special days for us.

Robby's brother, David, was six years older than Robby. David was an outstanding young man and dearly loved by everyone in Sanderson. Not just because he was "the Mayor's" boy, but because he was an extraordinary person. He was smart. He was personable. And, he was generous with his affections.

David's best friend was Roger Shinn. They were always together and always did the same things. They played football and basketball and both were stars. They were on the honor roll at Elkview High School. And they were popular with girls, which, at the time, did not impress either Robby or me.

Roger lived on Dutch Ridge and his home environment was very different from David's. His family was poor and uneducated. They never attended the church or came to any social events, except occasionally on Sanderson Days. Roger's dad drank a lot and was noted for being a drunk and a do-nothing. But Roger was determined to overcome his environment and he was doing a good job at it. He got along very well with the Robinsons and attended church regularly. He had a beautiful singing voice and sang solos and with groups. He could also give very good talks at midweek Testimony Meeting. He and David were co-teachers of the Boy's Bible Class, which Robby and I attended.

Robby liked Roger very much. In fact, with Roger, it almost seemed that the Robinsons had three children. Charlie Robinson said that

Roger, David, and Robby were "The Three Musketeers." They liked that name and even developed a little gesture to represent the way the Three Musketeers touched swords. They would raise their right hands and touch the ends of their index fingers.

When I was around, we were called the "Four Musketeers." I loved that. It made me feel special that these two older well-liked boys showered so much attention on Robby and me and included us in the things they did. They would often take an hour or two on Sunday afternoon to play games with us.

But as much as we liked them, we never invited them into one special area of our world. Although I'm sure they knew about our playground, we considered it our secret place.

Behind the Community Church was a knoll that had been cleared. Although it was not large, the knoll was almost flat. It belonged to Charlie Robinson and there was a rumor that he had planned to make it into a cemetery, but had changed his mind. The knoll, separated from Sanderson by tall oak trees, was our playground. We had a tire swing on a very long rope, a "fort" built out of old slab lumber we found, and a sandbox "town" with roads and houses where we played with our cars.

On one side of the clearing was a unique place that only Robby and I knew about. We called it our "Special Place." It was a thicket of Eastern Juniper trees, eight or ten feet tall, that grew very close together. The trees were prickly, but if you knew the special path, you could work your way into a small clearing inside the trees. The low growing limbs and the thickness of the Junipers make it impossible to see in or out.

One of the most unusual things about the little clearing inside the thicket was how it affected us. We became serious and secretive when we were in the Special Place. We would take a snack and go in and talk about things that were on our minds – the concerns of young boys, whatever they happened to be. While we enjoyed being the Four Musketeers when David and Roger joined us, we never shared the Special Place with them.

In 1950, the Korean War was on everyone's minds and it was the subject of more than one of our Special Place conversations. Robby was especially troubled by the war. He told me he didn't understand war and hated the thought of people killing each other. We played cowboys and carried our pearl handled six-shooter cap pistols, but war was different. It was terrible to think that boys from America were going there and getting killed.

Although I was aware of Robby's feelings about the war, I really didn't understand why he felt so strongly until the spring of 1951 – the spring David and Roger graduated from high school. It wasn't long after graduation that they announced they were joining the Army. They had a plan. While David's parents probably had the money to send him to college, there was no way that Roger could afford to go. The plan was that they would go into the Army; then, after they got out, they would both go to college on the GI Bill. Although they thought it was a good plan, no one else in Sanderson did, especially Robby.

On July 5, 1951, David and Roger left for boot camp. The day before, Sanderson Days, was a very strange day for Robby and me. I guess I really didn't understand how significant it was to Robby that David and Roger were going into the Army. Looking back on it now, I realize that he felt abandoned by them, but at the time, I was oblivious to his feelings. I was aware, however, of his behavior.

Robby became very moody that day. Instead of eating with everyone else, we spent most of the day at the playground. Nothing we did satisfied Robby. He didn't want to play cowboys. He didn't want to play cars. He didn't want to put the new boards we had found onto the fort. So, we spent our time in the Special Place, Robby sulking and lying on his back, staring up through the trees and not speaking.

Finally, he got very angry when I suggested we do something. He wanted to fight, so I crawled out of the Special Place and went down the hill and joined the group at Sanderson Days. I found David and Roger and sat near them. They were the center of attention and some of it splashed off on me. I liked that a lot better than having to deal with Robby's mood. Robby never did come down from the Special Place, and I went home without saying goodbye.

Robby and I continued to play together through the summer and into the fall, but it wasn't the same. David and Roger came home after finishing boot camp, and there was a party for them at the church before they shipped out. They were headed for Korea, a fact that seemed to weigh on everyone's mind, especially since the war had turned against us. President Truman had fired General MacArthur and everything about the war seemed gloomy. The people of Sanderson weren't eager to send their two best young men into that kind of situation.

The party was okay. But, it was obvious that David and Roger were very different. They stood straight and wore snappy uniforms. They were very serious and only smiled when I raised my hand with index finger pointed, to give the Four Musketeers salute. And instead of spending time with Robby and me, they went to visit kids they had gone to high school with. Then they were gone.

Needless to say, Robby's attitude didn't improve. He was no fun to be with. Robby's moods got so bad that I didn't look forward to going to church at Sanderson. Still, we tried to be friends. At times, Robby seemed determined to sabotage our friendship. He would be argumentative and feisty. At other times, he was his old self, the Robby I knew before David and Roger went to Korea. But, I never knew from one moment to the next which he was going to be.

After a while, I began to realize how David's leaving was affecting Robby. Having Sunday dinner at Robby's house and listening to his parents talk about the war didn't help Robby or me in the least. They were very pessimistic and often spoke openly of their fears that something might happen to David or Roger. These conversations always turned a happy playful Robby into a dark, moody, and fearful little boy. And I began to recognize words from these conversations as part of Robby's Special Place talks about the war.

Then, in the spring of 1952, Robby and I began to bond again. He seemed to be coming out of his depression and enjoying life. We relished the nice weather and every Sunday we were back at the knoll. But now, we expanded our adventures. We went exploring along the creek or climbed the hills and checked out all of the old sealed up coal mines. Things seemed to be getting better and Sundays were fun again.

Then, word came that Roger had been wounded in action. We didn't know the extent of his injuries, but they were said to be serious. He had been shot in the face, but he was expected to survive. Since his parents didn't associate with anyone in the area, it was difficult to get news on his condition.

I expected this news to drive Robby back into his moody shell. It did briefly, but he seemed to handle it okay. He seemed to be becoming a fatalist, accepting whatever came his way without question. However, his grades at school were suffering. There was talk of "holding him back a year," which, in those days, was a euphemism for failing.

In June, we heard that Roger was much better and would be coming home some time that fall. He was a hero and had been awarded the Purple Heart. When I tried to talk to Robby about Roger, he didn't want to hear it. From our Special Place conversations, I was beginning to see that Robby and his parents blamed Roger for talking David into joining the Army. If it weren't for Roger, David would be home, going to college right now. And, even if he had gotten drafted, he might not have gone to Korea.

In late June, two Army Chaplains came to Sanderson to tell Charlie, Marjorie, and Robby that David was missing in action. There were no details. What had happened and where it happened was all very secret. The Army would let them know more as soon as possible.

For the first time since it had started in the late 1930's, Sanderson Days was canceled. Instead, people met at the Community Church for a special time of prayer for David's safety. Rumors flew in all directions. David had been captured by the Chinese. David was on a secret mission and saying that he was missing in action was a cover. But, most people believed in their hearts that David was dead. Missing in action simply meant that they hadn't recovered his body.

Robby tried his best to act as if nothing had happened. He played harder than ever. In fact, he didn't want to stop playing. He wanted to run, he wanted to climb, he wanted to swing as high as possible. He became a daredevil and took chances climbing trees and rock cliffs that frightened me. He never mentioned David or the possibility that he was dead. It was as if he had no brother, just himself, and sometimes, me.

That fall, Roger Shinn came home to Sanderson. He was given a hero's welcome, but his return was overshadowed by that fact that there was no news about David. Roger had been shot in the face. The bullet had gone into his mouth and had taken out many of his teeth and his right jaw bone. The surgeons had done a very good job of reconstructive surgery and had replaced the jaw bone and even implanted teeth. However, because of skin grafts and damaged nerves, Roger's face was stiff and he couldn't smile. Also, the damage to his mouth and vocal cords made it almost impossible for Roger to talk. I should say, made it almost impossible for us to understand what Roger was saying.

I was visiting with Robby the day Roger came to see Charlie and Marjorie. They were cool to him at first, but as they talked, their attitude began to change and they started to accept what they had known all along, that going into the Army was not Roger's idea, but

David's. The Robinsons and Roger also knew that it was David's way of trying to help his best friend.

Robby and I sat with the Robinsons and listened to Roger. As long as he spoke slowly and deliberately, we could understand most of what he said. If he became emotional and began to cry, which he did often, we couldn't understand him at all. But even when he spoke deliberately, there were some words we couldn't make out. At times like these, Roger would write down what he was trying to say.

That fall, as we anxiously awaited word on David, Roger began to get back into the life of the community and the church. The church didn't have a minister, so Roger began to preach. It was a very trying experience for both him and the congregation. He was frustrated by the stiffness of his face and the damage to his mouth. He strained to make every word understandable, but most of the time his words were nasal and nearly impossible to understand.

In time, either he got better, or we began to understand him better, because it became less and less an ordeal.

Everyone, including the Robinsons, treated Roger with utmost respect and love except Robby. Robby's lack of respect wasn't a public thing, it was very private. I don't think anyone other than me knew how much he disliked Roger and wanted nothing to do with him. When we were alone in the Special Place or in the woods, Robby would mimic Roger's way of speaking. He actually became very good at it and on a number of occasions he would say something when I wasn't looking and I would turn expecting to see Roger.

Robby kept his distance from Roger, but not in a way that anyone other than Roger and I noticed. It was subtle and it was deliberate. Only the three remaining Musketeers were aware of the chasm that grew ever wider between Robby and Roger.

A year passed with no word about David. Charlie's attempts to learn more about his son were met with resistance. Peace negotiations were in progress and a settlement of the war seemed imminent. Important things were happening and no one seemed to have time to help a father looking for his missing-in-action son.

Sanderson Days, 1953, was a time of both hopefulness and continued worry. In late July, 1953, the armistice was signed at Panmunjom and the troops began coming home. There was still no word about David. To Sanderson, the loss of a native son was a great tragedy. But, in the big picture, David Robinson was only one of a million and a half soldiers who died in the war. He was just a statistic.

But to Robby, he was nothing – not even a memory. To mention David's name in his presence was, to Robby, like speaking a foreign language. He simply ignored any reference, any question, or any comment about his brother. He struggled on, filling his days with as many activities as possible, living in a fantasy world in which he was an only child.

In May, 1954, official word about David came in a telegram. He was dead. His "remains" would be returned to the United States. He was awarded a Purple Heart, posthumously, and he was eligible for burial at Arlington National Cemetery. But Charlie wanted his son home.

On Sunday, July 4, 1954, exactly three years after he and Roger had left for Basic Training, war hero David Allen Robinson was laid to rest in the small community cemetery in Sanderson, West Virginia, the town where he was born and where he lived all but about one year of his life.

The big Sanderson Days tent was used for the funeral because the church was too small to hold all of the people who came. The flag draped casket sat in state under the tent all morning as hundreds of friends, relatives, and curiosity seekers came by. At two o'clock, the funeral began. It lasted for two and a half hours.

Robby continued to ignore the fact that the funeral was for his brother. Because we were such good friends, the Robinsons allowed me to sit with them and Robby during the service. Every church in the area participated in the funeral. There were a lot of songs, by both the congregation and by soloists and groups. There were tributes by those who went to school with David. Poems were read. Prayers were offered. Three different ministers delivered "sermons" on the value of being a Christian which included vivid descriptions of your likely eternal abode if you put off making a decision this very moment.

Finally, Roger rose to speak. Instead of standing behind the podium, he stood beside the casket. Needless to say, he was very emotional. Each time he tried to speak, tears rolled down his cheeks. And when he did speak, no one could understand a word he was saying. Finally, he gave up and, leaning his head against the coffin, he began to sob and repeatedly uttered the only word that we had understood since he rose to speak: David.

We stood to pray. I could tell that Robby was very anxious by the way he kept squirming. As we stood with our heads bowed, waiting on Roger to gain control, Robby turned and looked at me. I'm embarrassed to tell you what I did next. I don't know why I did it, but I distorted my face and mimicked the look Roger has when he cries. To my surprise, Robby laughed. Actually, it was not a laugh, it was a loud snort.

He quickly turned away from me, but it was too late. He was out of control. He tried to stifle the laugh, but he couldn't. And neither could I! There we stood, trying hard not to laugh, but unable to keep from it. Our bodies shook and the air squirted as hisses between our teeth. Every eye in the place was on us.

I knew that I was dead. My mother would be totally humiliated and she would sacrifice me as an appeasement to the gods of proper funeral conduct. And I knew that Aunt Harriette would light the fire.

As I stood there, considering how far I might get before they caught me if I started running now, I began to sense that something else was going on under that tent. People did not know that we were laughing. They thought that we were crying. And the sight of two young grief stricken boys, one of them the brother of the deceased, was more than the hardest of hearts could bear. Everyone, even the most wicked, cruel, tobacco-chewing, snuff-dipping, moonshine drinking, unbathed coal miner who feared neither God nor man was sobbing like their hearts were broken. Marjorie reached out and placed her arm around Robby's shoulder and pulled him to her Maybe I wouldn't die after all.

From the tent, the casket was carried to the cemetery. There the ritual continued for another half hour. It was not until the casket was lowered into the ground and those in charge began to shovel the dirt into the grave that the crowd began to wander back toward the tent.

As was the custom, everyone stayed after the funeral and visited with the family. Food was served, and although it was not Sanderson Days, it began to become somewhat of a festive occasion. People began to smile and talk. Memories were shared and life began to return to a form of normalcy.

The food was served in the tent. But, as the day progressed and the sun beat down, the tent grew stifling, so some people moseyed over to the church which was cooler. At one point, Robby and I joined this group, and for reasons I never understood, Robby decided to do his Roger impersonation.

It began when we came in the door. Robby said something in his Roger voice and everyone turned around. They were puzzled to see the two of us. Someone asked where Roger was, and Robby answered in Roger's voice. A few people laughed, so Robby continued.

Robby did his best imitation of Roger giving a sermon, including a crying spell. Many found Robby's impersonation quite humorous and the more they laughed the more it encouraged Robby to continue.   Suddenly, everyone stopped laughing, but Robby was too caught up in the moment to notice. He kept up his imitation of Roger including facial distortions and gestures. But, I was aware that something was wrong and turned toward the door. There stood Roger. I punched Robby with my elbow to get him to stop. He looked at me and I motioned toward Roger.   Robby turned and stared at Roger. After a moment, Roger spoke.

"Robby," he said softly and plainly. "Can I talk to you for a minute?"

I could feel the tension in Robby. Suddenly he exploded. His words poured out.

Most of what he said was in incomplete and fragmented sentences.

"You're no preacher!" he shouted. "You just get up there and babble. No one can understand a word you're saying. You should stop pretending to be something you're not."

As he shouted at Roger, Robby began to cry. Finally he stopped. He stood there, his hands in fists, staring at Roger.

"I wish it was you!" he screamed. "I wish it was you!"

Then he turned and ran through the church and out the back door. Everyone sat stunned. Roger stood, looking in the direction that Robby had gone. Then he turned and left the church. I went through the church and out the back door to try to find Robby.

I looked everywhere for him. He was no place to be found. I checked the Special Place three times, but, no Robby. Finally, I heard my mom calling, so I left.

Things were never the same for Robby or Roger or me. Roger stopped preaching. He said that Robby was right. He was pretending to be something he wasn't. God had not called him to preach. It was just his way of showing his appreciation for not being killed. But instead, he was actually doing a disservice to God. Now, it was time for him to do what his best friend had wanted him to do; go to college as they had planned all along.

Robby went on pretending that he had no brother, or that David was not dead, or whatever it was that was going on in his head. He also refused to acknowledge that his outburst at Roger had ever happened. But, the dark moods returned and he became more aggressive and hostile toward everyone, including me.

At about the same time, our family started attending the Church of the Nazarene in Quick and we stopped going to the Sanderson Community Church. I didn't see Robby at all the rest of that summer. In the fall, I saw him at school, but things were very different. I was now in Junior High School, two grades ahead of him, and had a different circle of friends. Robby was a brooding and moody loner with no friends. I tried to talk with him when I could, but the Robby I used to know, my best friend and fellow Musketeer no longer resided behind the eyes I looked into when we spoke. He became a problem at school. He was always starting fights or creating disturbances. He refused to come to school for long periods until the Board of Education threatened his parents.

Still, there would be periods when he returned from where ever he went in his head and was the Robby I'd always known. During these times, which might last a month or more, we talked and had fun together. Then he'd go away again.

Roger started college. He studied business and accounting and made top grades.

He attended the Church of the Nazarene in Kanawha City, where he met a wonderful woman who really cared for him in spite of his disabilities. It wasn't long before they were going everywhere together, just like Roger and David. She listened patiently to him and when others couldn't understand what he was saying, she had the most gentle and unassuming way of telling them what Roger had said without making either Roger or the other person feel uncomfortable. She and Roger were married during his junior year in college.

The year Roger graduated from college at the top of his class Robby turned 16 and quit school. Robby hung around home for a while, arguing with his parents and creating as many problems as he could. Then one day, he left. He took only a few belongings and a little money and disappeared.

Roger worked for several different companies during the first five years after he graduated from college. He was successful in each case, and moved on when better offers came his way. Finally, he decided to open his own business. He was an almost instant success. People loved Roger and his attitude toward life. They conspired to make him successful by giving or sending him business. He rose to leadership in the state chapter of the Disabled American Veterans. He was prominent in his community and in his church. He was written about in a national magazine. He became wealthy and he was generous.

For ten years, no one knew if Robby was dead or alive. When Charlie died of a heart attack, they didn't know where to find Robby to let him know his dad was dead.

Then, in the late 1960s, Robby surfaced. In fact, the very same year Roger was being nationally recognized for his successes, Robby was being nationally recognized also.

I learned later from Robby that for the first five years after he quit school and left Sanderson, he just bummed around. He was arrested for shoplifting a couple of times and served some jail time for one offense. Then, while working as a night dishwasher at a fancy restaurant in Los Angeles, he saw some young successful patrons who were about his age. They were well-dressed, well-groomed, and having an enjoyable evening. In an instant, he made the decision that he was going to change his way of living. He talked the manager into letting him work as a waiter. He made very good money. He enrolled at a community college and was able to get a GED, then began taking college courses. But as hard as he tried, he could not shake the dark moods that came to haunt him. He had no friends. He was a loner and a failure.

But he kept trying. Finally, after two years at the community college he decided to try his hand at a state school. He enrolled at the University of California at Berkeley. Here he found his calling. Not in the academic world, but in the social underworld.

Berkeley was quickly becoming a hot bed of defiance. Protests against the war in Vietnam were daily occurrences. Here was something that Robby could believe in – the antiwar movement. He was quickly accepted and rose to leadership among the dissidents. And that's when he surfaced on national television and the front pages of newspapers across the country. There he was, my old pal Robby Robinson, burning an American flag – holding the staff and defiantly waving our flaming national symbol toward the camera as if he were waving it under all of our noses!

In 1970, I saw Robby again for the first time since he quit school and disappeared. I was living in Kansas City, working as a film editor for a local television station. Robby was in town to lead a march against the war. He was the chief national organizer and was working with a number of local people to get permission for the march and to ensure a good turn out.

I don't know how he knew I was in Kansas City, but the phone rang one night, and it was Robby. We met for lunch the next day and he filled me in on his reason for being in Kansas City. He was very intense and very upbeat, and I easily recognized the persona of the Robby I knew before his world fell apart.

He had to rush off after lunch, but we set a time to have dinner and talk. The march was the next day. Everything was arranged, so that night he was both relaxed and tense at the same time. He was in a very good mood and was expecting a good demonstration with little or no problems. We talked and talked and talked. Actually, I listened and listened and listened.

He began talking in a detached manner about his schooling and his leadership role in the antiwar movement. He didn't feel that he was opposing the war in Vietnam, but that he was opposing *all* war. He was demonstrating against wars past, wars present, and wars to come. His work had eternal significance.

As he talked, his speech was full of the clichés of the day. No more war. Give peace a chance. Stop the insanity.

But after a while he began to tell me about his life since he left Sanderson. He told me how shocked he was when he found out that both his dad and mom were dead. He made a "secret" trip back to Sanderson to visit their graves. He talked about the problems, the demons, the black moods, and how he was trying to turn his life around. He would complete his degree within the next year or two. He was toying with becoming a lawyer so he could be in a better position to fight the evils in society and help the disenfranchised. Right now, he was majoring in psychology and clinical counseling.

Then we talked about the days before he left Sanderson, about the Special Place and all of the fun we'd had together. Robby was so alive and so full of positive energy that it amazed me, but the more we talked about life in Sanderson, the more I could see the darkness creep in.

During the whole time, he never mentioned Roger, but he did talk about David. It was the strangest conversation. He talked about David as if he were someone Robby had heard about, but did not know personally. He was very objective, without even the slightest hint that this "David" was a real person, let alone his brother and a fellow Musketeer. When I saw the direction Robby's mood was beginning to take, I changed the subject.

The next day was the march. Robby asked me to walk with him in the demonstration. I had my own feelings about the war and I was dealing with it in a very different way from Robby. Over the past three or four years, I had spent a lot of time with men and women who very much believed in America's role in Vietnam, but who lived in daily dread that the young men they loved, their children, who were soldiers in that war, might not return. As I talked with these parents, I thought of Charlie and Marjorie Robinson and the fears they must have known.

But, for old time's sake, I walked with Robby. We must have made an interesting pair, he in his costume and me in mine. But we walked down Broad Street toward downtown Kansas City, arm-in-arm, chanting, waving, singing, and flashing the peace sign at the police who lined the way, while many of them smiled and flashed the peace sign back to us.

Now, two years later, flashing a peace sign at these six crazed young men standing menacingly in front of us was the last thing I had on my mind.

The ring leader continued to glare at Robby.

"Okay," Robby said softly. "We'll go."

We stood, and as we did, a soft familiar voice spoke.

"You two aren't going anywhere until we've had a chance to catch up on old time."

It was Roger. I turned toward him. His face was stiff, but his eyes were smiling. The young men who had confronted us now turned their glare to Roger.

"You're going to talk to him, after what he done?"

An exasperated look came over Roger's face.

"How many times does it have to be said that America is a free country? Have you ever heard of the Constitution? The Bill or Rights? Freedom?" I was amazed at the clarity of Roger's voice, how easily I understood every word.

"We have freedom," Roger continued. "This is not Communist Russia or Red China. We don't rule by mob and by intimidation in America. He has as much right to do what he's doing as you and I have to do what we're doing."

"But, he burned the flag of our country!"

"Let me ask you something. How many of you ever served in the military?"

The boys stared at Roger; a couple of them looked down.

"How many of you have ever been wounded fighting for this country."

The group began to fidget.

"How many of you ever had a brother killed in action?"

I saw Robby stiffen. The boys all began to look down or away to avert Roger's eyes.

"None of you. Well, you're looking at two men who suffered a great loss because of war and that gives us the right to speak our minds on the subject; me my way and him his way.

"Besides, the only reason you're standing here is that your number didn't come up in the draft. I've heard your stories, every one of them. I've heard you brag about how you didn't have to go. The war is still going on. Every one of you is of fighting age. I happen to personally know the Army and Marine recruiters. I can put in a good word for you if you'd like to go to Vietnam."

The boys began to look a little sheepish. Then, as a group, they turned and walked away.

"Hello, Roger," I said. It's good to see you."

We laughed. I shook Roger's hand. Then he and Robby shook hands. It was a warm, friendly handshake. The three of us stood and talked for a while. It was polite conversation made up mostly of how are you's with little or no mention of what we all wanted most to talk about. After a while, Roger told us both how nice it was to see us and slipped away.

Robby and I wandered through the tent toward the outside. People smiled at Robby now and spoke to him by name. Roger had made him more acceptable. I know that everyone was curious about his life, but no one dared to ask.

We walked up the road to the Community Church and went inside. Robby did not speak. He just stood there among the memories. After a while, we made our way down the aisle and out the side door.

The path to our playground was grown over, but we had walked it so many times that we automatically followed where it had been.

The playground had changed. The grass was tall and small trees now filled the area that had once been cleared. The rope still hung from the tree, but the tire in which we swung was gone. We found only a few rotten remnants of the fort and no sign at all of the little village with its roads and houses. But the Special Place was unchanged.

We crawled through the thicket and stood inside. It seemed small now, but we knew that, actually, it was mostly the same size as when we were kids. We did not speak. We just listened to the echoes of all the talks we had there over the years. The Robby who hated war was born in this thicket. We both knew that now.

We left the playground and made our way through the woods to the cemetery. Robby led the way as we visited his dad's grave, then his mom's, then David's. Robby stood quietly for a few moments, looking down at his brother's grave. Then he moaned. It was an awful sound and I thought he was dying. He sagged, and then dropped to the ground on his knees. He leaned forward over his brother's grave and began to pound the ground with his fist.

"Why?" he asked, his voice full of anger. "Why did you do this to me? I needed you. I needed a brother. Why did you have to do this *to me*?"

I knelt on the ground beside him, but was afraid to touch him. He was panting as if he had been running and the sound he made worried me. Then I heard the snap of a twig. I looked across the cemetery toward the entrance to see Roger coming toward us. He had his head down, picking his way through the tall grass. Robby had seen him too.

Roger took a few more steps before he looked up. He stopped when he saw us.

"I'm sorry," he said. "I didn't know."

He stood for a moment, and then turned to leave.

"Roger," called Robby.

Roger turned back toward us.

"Please," said Robby. "Come join us."

Roger came to the grave and knelt on the other side, opposite Robby and me. We looked down at the grave as if looking into David's open coffin. No one spoke for a minute or two.

"Roger," Robby said, looking up at him. "I'm sorry."

Roger nodded.

"I'm sorry for what I said at the funeral and for all the pain it might have caused you."

Roger tried to smile, but his face wouldn't let him. "It's okay," he said softly.

The two men continued to look at each other across David's grave. I could see tears beginning to form in Roger's eyes."

"That day," he said and we all knew what day he was talking about. "That day when I asked to talk with you, I wanted to tell you something about David.

"When we joined up, we had big plans. We would go to war. We would help win the war. We could come home. We would get our college degrees. We would own a business together. We would be rich."

He sighed.

"We had our plans.

"When we signed up, we said that we wanted to be together all the time. The recruiter assured us it would be no problem. That was the first lie they told us. After basic, we only saw each other once.

"It was a cold December evening. We were high in the mountains in north central

Korea. The war was going against us. The brass wouldn't admit it, but we all knew.

"Our units crossed paths and we were camped in the same area for one night. David and I spent the evening together, talking. We still had our plans, but now we weren't so sure. We'd seen too much and we were beginning to lose faith. So David asked me to promise him something."

Roger stopped, fighting back tears, then continued.

"He said, 'Roger, if I don't make it back, be a brother to Robby.'

"That day, when I came in the church to find you, I wanted to tell you about the promise."

We were silent. I was afraid that Roger would start to cry, but he didn't. And Robby was calm, calmer than he had been in a long time.

"Every time I go to church, I think of that scripture that says that if you come to worship and remember that your brother has something against you, leave your gift and go find your brother and make it right. I would have done that if I had known where to find you.

"And over the years, I have prayed that one day I'd be able to keep my promise to David and be the brother to you that he would have been."

Robby looked down at the grave for a long moment, then back up at Roger.

"Roger," he said. "Today God has answered your prayers."

The two reached across the grave and put their arms around each other. They were laughing and crying at the same time, and so was I. Reconciliation! It's a wonderful feeling.

After a while, we stood, dusted our knees, and turned to look at the monument at the head of David's grave. Then we turned to each other. As we were about to leave, I impulsively raised my right hand, the index finger pointing upward, in a Musketeer's salute. And automatically the other two touched their fingers to mine.

The Four Musketeers, together again!

Made in the USA
Lexington, KY
09 September 2013